THE ARRANGEMENT

A Gunter Wayan Private Investigator Thriller

ALAN REFKIN

THE ARRANGEMENT
A GUNTER WAYAN PRIVATE INVESTIGATOR THRILLER

iUniverse books may be ordered through booksellers or by contacting:

iUniverse
1663 Liberty Drive
Bloomington, IN 47403
www.iuniverse.com
844-349-9409

ISBN: 978-1-6632-3408-7 (sc)
ISBN: 978-1-6632-3409-4 (e)

Library of Congress Control Number: 2021925683

Print information available on the last page.

iUniverse rev. date: 12/29/2021

To my wife, Kerry

and

Meir Daller, MD

PROLOGUE

October 20, 2021—4:40 a.m. in the Arabian Sea near the Yemeni island of Socotra

Gunter Wayan and Eka Endah were running for their lives. Unarmed, they wove through the maze-like corridors as two North Korean men with AK-47s gave chase, bullets flying past and peppering the walls and floor inches from their bodies. They didn't have a clue in hell where they were going. They were trying to stay alive and escape their captors.

The Indonesian private investigators were in decent shape, more so than the seamen trying to kill them. That became apparent the more prolonged the chase ensued, the gunfire decreasing as their pursuers dropped further behind. Five minutes after they dodged the last salvo, they saw a ladder that went to the deck above and took it.

As they stepped off the top rung, their mouths went agape. They were unprepared for what they saw. They were standing on an abandoned oil platform with nothing but water visible from horizon to horizon. More surprising were the five massive ICBMs sitting on mobile launch pads. Connected to each missile were two eight-inch steel tubes wrapped with thick metallic insulation. Each branched to the missile from a different separator, which received whatever it was pumping from somewhere below deck. The steel tubes were extremely cold given the quarter-inch layers of ice that surrounded their entries into the ICBMs.

"They're getting ready to launch these bad boys," Wayan said.

"It looks that way. That begs the question of why they brought us here."

"I think this was a scheduled stop for the ship before they kidnapped us, and we weren't meant to see the platform or the missiles. If we didn't escape, we'd still be locked in our cabin and have no idea about any of this."

Wayan turned and saw one of the seamen who was chasing them come out of a hatch fifty yards to the rear. The man shouldered and aimed his AK-47 assault rifle, which could discharge bullets at eleven rounds per second. They were the definition of the walking dead. However, he didn't fire. Wayan wasn't about to ask for an explanation and grabbed Eka's hand and ran towards an ICBM, not about to overthink the situation and give the young seaman a chance to reassess pulling the trigger.

"He didn't shoot," Eka said in wonderment.

"I'm guessing the only reason we're alive is that this missile was behind us and being fueled," he responded, trying to keep up with her. "If one of his rounds missed and hit it, we'd all be plucking a harp."

With the seaman running towards them and trying to get a clear shot, they found themselves being herded by him away from the missile and to the right corner of the platform. Not wanting to go for a swim, they took the only option available and scrambled down a ladder leading to the deck below. Taking successive down ladders, they continued their descent until they reached the superstructure deck, where the ship on which they were imprisoned was docked. Two vessels were berthed at adjacent docks.

"How long do you think we have before they look on this deck?" Eka asked.

"They'll want to search every room on each deck to ensure they don't miss us. At least, that's what I'd do. Judging from the size of the platform, we should have around an hour, and that assumes someone doesn't see us while boarding or coming off one of these ships."

The ship docked directly in front of them, which flew the Iranian flag, was the Bahri Ghazal—the name painted in thick white letters on the vessel's bow. Protruding from its deck were two large, insulated steel tubes—the same type connected to the missiles. The steel tubes extended to the platform and were attached to circular junction boxes, each with a cutoff wheel. They exited these boxes at a ninety-degree angle and ran along the exterior of the platform to the upper deck.

"What do you want to do?" Eka asked.

"What I want will probably get us killed."

"You want to destroy those missiles."

"Think about it. They're fueling five huge ICBMs for launch on what appears to be a deserted oil and gas platform in the middle of the ocean. These aren't test flights. A lot of people are going to die when they reach their targets."

"I saw Hangul lettering along the sides of the missiles," Eka said, referring to letters from the Korean alphabet. "That makes them North Korean."

"Which makes sense since they kidnapped us," Wayan added. "I think I know where the missiles are going."

"Israel."

Wayan nodded in agreement. "The Iranian flagged ship that's pumping fuel to them means Iran is involved. I can't see them fueling missiles owned by North Korea unless it's to their benefit. If Kim Jong-un could transport the missiles here, he could also bring the fuel. Therefore, why get it from Iran and risk exposing whatever he planned? That makes me believe he sold them to Iran to get hard currency."

"Israel will respond by taking out the country's military bases and leveling their nuclear research and storage facilities. They'll also destroy Iran's oil industry, which will drive it into bankruptcy in no time."

"That's the response I'd expect if these missiles are carrying conventional warheads. If they're nuclear-tipped with a MIRV," he said, referring to a multiple independent reentry vehicle, "then Israel will be decimated and won't be able to respond."

"And Iran can deny any knowledge of the attack because the missile tracks will show they were launched from whatever ocean we're in and not the Islamic republic," Eka added.

"Israel has a lot of enemies. Iran will claim the attack was by one of them. Without proof, who's to say it didn't? Both countries will chew on each other in the United Nations, but that's all that will come of it."

"That brings us to the question of how we destroy these missiles."

"We start a fire," Wayan said. "That will ignite the missiles and send the platform to the floor of the ocean."

"Along with us."

"Not if escape by borrowing one of these ships."

"That might work. How do we start the fire?"

"We break the glass, take a flare gun," Wayan said, pointing to a pair in a steel box affixed to a support beam, "and send the flare into a fuel tube. The fire will ignite the fuel all the way to the missiles. Boom."

"We'll be in the center of that boom because the fuel ship behind us will explode," Endah countered.

"Not if we cut off the fuel at the circular junction boxes and ignite one of the fuel ducts on the other side of it. I'll wrap my jacket around my hands. The vapor coming from the ice encrusting the cutoff wheel looks cold enough to give me frostbite and pull the skin off."

"It would," a voice said.

Startled, they looked to their right and saw a man five feet, five inches in height, with piercing black eyes and a patch of black stubbles trying to break the surface near the rear of his head. With a 12-gauge shotgun in his hands, he looked at them in the brutal way a predator saw its prey.

"That's an excellent plan. The missiles are being fueled with liquid hydrogen, which leaves this ship at minus four hundred twenty-three degrees Fahrenheit," Jae-Hwa Ock said, nodding toward the Iranian vessel. "The other large conduit is delivering liquid oxygen, which is the oxidizer. It's at minus two hundred ninety-eight degrees Fahrenheit. Touching either of the cutoff wheels on the junction boxes with your bare skin would give you frostbite and a serious burn."

"I guess it's time to return to our cabin," Wayan said, raising his hands. Eka also put her hands in the air.

"Unfortunately, that's not an option," the man replied as he raised the shotgun to eye-level and fired twice in rapid succession.

The force of the blasts hurled Wayan and Eka backward. They landed hard and were motionless on the metal deck.

The man walked to the bodies and kicked them to ensure he didn't receive a response. It was over.

CHAPTER 1

Twenty-six years earlier—1995

The island was eight hundred miles off the coast of Mumbai, India. Once a British prison, they abandoned it in 1895 because of the immense cost of transporting and housing prisoners so far from shore. It appeared on mariners' maps as Scops Island—named by an early explorer who observed that the reddish-brown Scops owl species was abundant throughout most of the island's six thousand four hundred acres, eighty-six percent of which was jungle. In the century since the British left and put it up for sale, the jungle reclaimed what they hacked from it and engulfed every structure and clearing—erasing all evidence of human habitation.

In 1995, a multi-billionaire Indian technology entrepreneur attended a party and heard about the island from an international real estate broker. The entrepreneur, acknowledged by most of his colleagues as eccentric, became intrigued by the history of Scops Island. He particularly liked its closeness to Mumbai—his primary domicile and the headquarters for his company. Impulsively deciding to see it, he left the party, real estate broker in tow, and went there on his two hundred and fifty million dollars, three hundred feet yacht.

When they arrived at the island, he and the broker discovered the dock had deteriorated and that only the pilings were visible above the water. Therefore, the captain anchored as close to the beach

1

as he dared. The entrepreneur, the real estate broker, and several crewmembers came ashore in a raft. However, since no one thought to bring a machete or one of the ship's drones, all they could do was look at the dense jungle from the sand beach. They returned to the yacht.

They were better prepared when they came ashore and launched a pair of drones with video cameras the following day. Three hours later, they completed their survey of the ten-square-mile island. All they saw were tropical trees and dense undergrowth. Evidence of the century-old buildings which once housed prisoners, guards, and support staff was undetectable, having been swallowed by the jungle.

Upon returning to the ship, the real estate broker went to the bar and began to self-medicate with three fingers of Johnny Walker Blue—feeling certain the entrepreneur wouldn't purchase the property. She was wrong. Approaching her after the steward poured a second medicinal dose of scotch, he said Scops Island was precisely what he wanted—a bastion of extreme privacy away from the urban annoyances of Mumbai. It would give him more time to create new products while running his tech empire remotely using a satellite link for audio, visual, and data communications. Because he was a billionaire, he also liked the remoteness insulating him from those who constantly sought favors and money.

The closing took less than a week, after which the entrepreneur opened the money spigot to transform the island into his residence. The contractors, architects, engineers, electricians, and other specialties took two years to complete their plans. One-and-a-half-billion dollars lighter, and five years later, the entrepreneur spent his first night on Scops Island.

The island boasted an eight thousand feet runway and adjoining hangar, warehouses, a cargo dock with heavy loading and unloading capabilities, an array of satellite antennas and associated whiz-bang technical equipment, a desalination plant, a large-scale solar farm, several immense backup generators, and a wastewater treatment plant. His residence was on par with his palatial home on Mumbai's

Malabar Hill. The twenty thousand square feet, two-story house, just as every building on the island, was constructed of reinforced concrete and designed to withstand a category five hurricane. Fifty yards to the right of the residence were a dozen villas for senior support personnel. A similar distance to the left were two, three-story buildings for the other one hundred fifty full-time staff. Everything went smoothly for the next seven years, and the entrepreneur's tech empire continued to grow until a cataclysmic event shook the world.

September 21, 2009

With the global financial crisis, the banks transformed their business model. Lending was no longer in their lexicon. Instead, they focused on getting their money back and cutting their exposure to highly leveraged clients and industries that lacked hard assets. The entrepreneur, who for decades received bank loans to fuel his cash-intensive business, suddenly found himself cut off from capital and put on notice that he would need to speed up repaying his loans. He contemplated doing a sale-leaseback of his company campus to repay the bank, after which he'd tell them to twirl on it. He'd done this type of transaction several times before with other properties. However, with real estate worth less than twenty percent of its value six months ago, nobody wanted to touch a sale-leaseback transaction until the market bottomed out—an unknown timeline. Subsequently, he put his real estate portfolio, yacht, jet, and Scops Island on the market to get whatever money he could.

Three weeks after the property was listed, his broker received a call from an attorney who said he had a client willing to purchase it for three hundred million dollars—substantially less than the five hundred million dollars asking price. Desperate for the cash to save his company, the entrepreneur countered at four hundred million and a no-contingency close, indicating that cannibalizing and selling the equipment would bring in almost that much, and the runway alone cost one hundred fifty-five million dollars. Going back and forth for several days, the attorney for the buyer, who he would only say was an offshore corporation, agreed to those terms.

Three weeks after the property purchase, and for several years after that, the buyer began an extensive underground construction project. Since Scops Island was off the radar of virtually every intelligence agency, there were no spy satellites, aerial reconnaissance flights, or marine electronic surveillance of what occurred there. Three years and two months later, a five-story, one hundred twenty-five thousand square feet underground research facility became operational. Although the spec of land in the Arabian Sea was still identified as Scops Island on maritime charts, North Korea referred to it as Facility Number One. Designed to produce nuclear warheads and medium and long-range missiles, the hermit Kingdom secretly transported these weapons, away from the prying eyes of nations sanctioning them, back to the homeland and to its largest client—Iran.

October 1, 2021

The Gulfstream G450 was fueled and ready for takeoff from the executive air terminal of the Macau International Airport. Bikas Tsang sat in the left seat and impatiently drummed the fingers of his left hand on his armrest. It was nine a.m., an hour past their scheduled departure time, and his co-pilot, Tobias Poy, hadn't shown. Under normal circumstances, a client who was paying thousands an hour for the charter, along with the company's operations center, would chew his ass to get in the air. However, since they were transporting cargo, and the contract didn't specify when it must arrive, the director of operations gave them substantial leeway.

Tsang had a good idea where Poy was because they stayed in the same hotel and sat next to each other at the downstairs bar the night before. That partnership lasted until ten when Poy, a skirt chaser first-class, hit on an EVA flight attendant. Two drinks later, they were passionately kissing and had their hands wrapped around each other. Shortly after that, he paid the tab and left with her. Judging from his co-pilot's lateness, he had difficulty leaving the attractive brunette and getting his ass to the aircraft.

It was ten-fifteen a.m. when Poy raced out of the terminal and stepped aboard the Gulfstream.

"Sorry I'm late," he said, although the smile on his face and the tone of his voice showed otherwise.

"Get any sleep?"

"None," Poy answered with a grin.

"BCN on. Parking brake set. Power levers idle. Gust lock off," Tsang stated as he began going down the engine start checklist. "I hope you have the same luck in Cebu," he said with a smile, referring to their destination.

The Mactan-Cebu International Airport was in the Philippines, one thousand one hundred miles from Macau. Tsang and Poy lived in Hong Kong and worked as a team for an international VIP transport and freight company. They were requested by name to fly marine electronic equipment to a stranded yacht in Cebu and told by operations that the boxed components secured in the rear of their aircraft were replacing those fried when lightning struck the yacht. Neither knew who requested them, each surmising that they must have at some time transported the owner of the yacht, and he liked their performance.

"Now is as good a time as any to confess that the lady you saw with me at the bar has a girlfriend who's also a flight attendant—and single."

"Engine Bleed Air off. Main boost pumps on. Engine control to EPR mode," Tsang said, continuing down the checklist. "I'm not sure that's much of an endorsement if she told you about her girlfriend," he said as he watched the readings on the LED screen.

"She didn't tell me about her. She invited her to my room."

"You were with two women? You had my room number. We're a team."

"Which I selfishly ignored. You would have too if you saw her friend."

"Bleed air pressure is above thirty-two PSI. TGT is less than two hundred degrees centigrade. Start master on. Turning the starboard engine. Fuel Control to run," Tsang stated, nodding with satisfaction at the engine readings that appeared on the LED screen. He placed his hand on the left throttle to begin the same procedures for the port engine. At that instant, a digital timer in one of the cargo boxes reached zero, sending an electronic impulse to a detonator inside a brick of C-4 explosive. The aircraft, which carried two hundred ninety-four thousand five hundred pounds of highly flammable JP-4 fuel, exploded and sent a fireball and pieces of the plane over one hundred feet into the air. The concussive force that followed shattered every window and sliding glass door within the executive air terminal, less than thirty yards away, and reduced the forty million dollar aircraft to twisted and burnt pieces of scrap.

Ten minutes earlier

Jae-Hwa Ock watched the G450 from the observation deck above the main terminal of the Macau International Airport, incessantly checking his watch and deducing how much time remained until the Gulfstream exploded. He didn't understand why the second pilot wasn't there. All he knew was that the timer he'd placed in the crate that was now aboard the aircraft couldn't be reset. He realized he'd made a mistake assuming that paying an exorbitant amount of money to charter the Gulfstream and requesting Tsang and Poy as the crew would guarantee the plane left Macau at the time given to him by the scheduler. Instead, he should have specified when the aircraft needed to be in Cebu. But that was now water under the bridge, and all he could do was hope the second pilot was on board within the next ten minutes. As much as he would have liked to know if that happened and watch the explosion, he needed to leave. Ock rushed off the observation deck and down the concrete stairway. He was halfway across the parking lot when he heard the explosion. He should have left earlier because he needed to get off the airport property before the police cordoned it and questioned everyone within its boundaries. Three minutes after he left the parking lot, the police did exactly that.

During the thirty-five mile drive to Shenzhen's Bao'an International Airport in China, Ock slammed his fist on the steering wheel in frustration. If the aircraft had only left on time, the explosion would have occurred over the Luzon strait, beneath which was an eight thousand five hundred feet trench that ran between Taiwan and the Philippines. It would be challenging to find the aircraft in those deep waters, and without the black boxes containing the cockpit voice recordings and flight data, there would be no reason to suspect a bomb caused the crash. Instead, the assumption would be there was a catastrophic aircraft malfunction. However, instead of the innocuous deaths of Tsang and Poy, he had a public spectacle. It wouldn't be long before the government would begin investigating their deaths and who was behind them.

October 4, 2021

The Sydney Kingsford Smith Airport, colloquially referred to as the Sydney airport, was built in 1919. Located five miles from the center of Sydney and wedged between urban growth on three sides and Botany Bay on the fourth, it was the twelfth busiest airport in the world.

Rizal Radisti, and his co-pilot Harto Fauzi, had just finished transporting the twenty-eight-year-old prima donna wife of a Malaysian industrialist from Kuala Lumpur to Sydney—a distance of four thousand one hundred twelve miles. Long before their aircraft landed, they were ready to set it down on any island along their flight path that had a runway and toss her off the plane. Had they not been over open water, they might have done just that. Nothing they did seemed to appease the Botox-Juvéderm princess. She complained about everything, from the brand of Champagne and the temperature at which they served it to the fact that the caviar came from Russia and not Iran—in her estimation, a faux pas of enormous magnitude. The cabin temperature was also one of her hot buttons. According to her, the elevated temperature within the main cabin was intolerable. The pilot responded by explaining that he had a digital control in the cockpit by which he could set the precise temperature in the main cabin. A self-test of that system showed it was working flawlessly. However, the prima donna angrily refused to accept this explanation and his suggestion that she might be cooler if she removed the heavy sweater over her blouse. This comment moved her temper dial to the nuclear position, setting off a tirade. After that, every thirty minutes or so during the rest of the flight, she issued gruff commands to lower or raise the temperature. For nearly eight hours, the flight attendant and crew endured these and numerous other complaints from the industrialist's fifth wife. Upon landing and an exceedingly fast taxi to the VIP terminal, the crew couldn't get the prima donna and her baggage off the aircraft and into the waiting limousine quick enough.

Once she was on her way, the flight attendant declared she would go to the hotel and stay in her room to decompress until their flight to Hong Kong the following day. The pilot and co-pilot, determining that alcohol was a better remedy for decompression, said they would take a taxi to the bar across the street from the airport. Their usual Sydney watering hole was popular with arriving aircrews, giving them a forty percent discount on all drinks.

Jae-Hwa Ock was seated at the counter of the Sydney watering hole, pushing around the same drink that he'd been served an hour ago, when he saw Radisti and Fauzi enter at eight p.m. He knew they'd be here from an investigative agency report he commissioned, which showed they always stopped here to have one or more drinks before going to their hotel. The information also included their flight schedule.

The agency which tracked Radisti and Fauzi was one of several Ock hired to locate everyone involved, even tangentially, in stealing money from his employer. He compiled eight names from their reports, including the pilots who provided air transport out of the country for those who carried out the theft. His employer's instructions were to orchestrate the deaths of four of the six people targeted to appear as innocuous as possible. Two would perish in a mishap—the ultimate cause of their death a mystery. The last two, he needed alive.

Since the first deaths hadn't gone as planned, and his employer eviscerated him over the phone for the public spectacle, he needed better luck with the remaining four. His employer didn't believe in forgiveness. Instead, he believed in replacing those who failed him by putting a bullet into their head, or worse, and getting someone else to take over.

Both pilots took a seat at the counter, their preferential place to sit, parking themselves ten feet to Ock's left. Waiting until they'd received their drinks, he got off his barstool and, as one of the pilots was taking a sip, bumped into him hard enough to cause the drink to spill. He immediately apologized for his clumsiness and bought both pilots another round. As the bartender put them on the counter, he picked them up and handed them to the pilots, dropping a pill he held between the index and middle fingers into each. The tiny tablets dissolved immediately in the dark liquid.

The poison dropped into the drinks would reach its apex of deadliness in six hours—when both men would hopefully be asleep. The chemicals introduced into their bodies would make it appear they died of paralytic shellfish poisoning, for which there is no antidote. PSP occurs when someone consumes seafood that has bioaccumulated toxins produced by microalgae. Shellfish with this bioaccumulation don't taste different from those that are non-lethal, and neither cooking nor freezing will destroy the toxins. The only protection for the consumer is a test for toxins conducted by licensed harvesters. In Australia, PSP is well-known to coroners and forensic technicians. The plan worked. At two a.m. Radisti and Fauzi's muscles became paralyzed from the effects of the poison on their nervous systems, duplicating what occurred from the ingestion of the shellfish toxin. They died within minutes of one another at approximately three-fifteen a.m. By this time, Ock was on his way to Shanghai, China, an intermediate stop before returning to Pyongyang and briefing his employer—Kim Jong-un, the supreme leader of the Democratic People's Republic of Korea.

CHAPTER 2

October 6, 2021

Langit Tamala was six feet, five inches tall with close-cut brown hair, brown eyes, medium brown skin, and a wedged-shaped upper torso that was not unlike a swimmer. A major in the Kopassus, the Indonesian army's special forces, he was stationed at the Halim Air Base in East Jakarta, which was on the opposite side of the runway from the civilian airport. His second in command was Captain Bakti Nabar, the special force's martial arts instructor. Nabar was bald, six feet, one inch tall with light brown skin, hazel eyes, and a thick muscular torso giving the impression to anyone who might be stupid enough to punch him in the torso that he wouldn't feel it.

Those in the military know there are three parts to military life. The first is the restlessness and boredom created when waiting for operational deployment. The second is the constant exercises designed to keep everyone sharp and iron out kinks in performance and strategy. The third is deployment, where errors in judgment, bad intel, or encountering a superior force could mean, unlike a practice exercise, coming home in a body bag rather than attending an after-exercise critique.

Tamala's six-man team was "enjoying" the second part of military life, having stepped off a helicopter and walking into the dense jungle on the Indonesian archipelago of Sumbawa. Their mission was to rescue a hostage held by terrorists.

"Too bad we don't have time for you to see your father," Tamala said to Nabar, speaking into his headset mic. "How close is his farm?"

"Just to the left of the landing zone. As a kid, I watched special forces teams land and go into the jungle. It was exciting to a farm boy and the reason I joined the army."

"Not much of a farmer?"

"I don't have the patience. When you're a farmer, you're bound to the land. It's not like you can take a vacation and leave the crops unattended. In some ways, it's like taking care of children."

"Ever come in here?" Tamala asked, referring to the jungle side of the archipelago, which was in stark contrast to the massive clearings where the farmers grew their crops.

"I'd sneak in once in a while and catch hell from my father when I came out." The two broke off their conversation when they entered an especially dense area of undergrowth.

While civilians might think of a trek through the jungle as a tranquil nature walk within a picturesque landscape, those in the military have a differing point of view. The reason was that military jungle training exercises and operational missions were in environments where most of what walked, crawled, or slithered viewed anything living as part of the food chain or something they should kill to protect themselves.

Kopassus special forces teams were often dropped into the dense jungle, hacking through while carrying backpacks weighing forty-five pounds plus. The Sumbawa site was one of a multitude the government owned throughout the country, also letting other countries use these to train their special forces. The common denominator with every site was that, once inside the jungle, it was difficult for the teams to call the outside world because the thick canopy of trees blocked radio frequency and satellite communications. To contact someone, they needed to see a patch of sky, which usually meant someone shimming to the top of a tree and planting an antenna.

The military didn't hire a luxury excursion company such as Abercrombie and Kent to handle their deployments. Soldiers were expected to survive on what they carried, live off the land, and compete for food and water with the same life forms trying to kill them. Lumping the entire experience together, those who took part in jungle training exercises referred to it as green hell.

Tamala's team was on their way to a shack four miles, as the crow flew, from their current position. The purpose of this exercise was to rescue an abducted business executive—a role played by a Kopassus lieutenant, who was being held there by local terrorists. The going was tough as the team sliced their way through heavy vegetation and thick vines. Four hours and twenty minutes after they left their transport, they found the shack and saw four perimeter security guards patrolling the area around it.

Every soldier on this exercise used a MILES, short for Multiple Integrated Laser Engagement System. This was a collection of small sensors scattered over the body. When a laser beam from a weapon struck one, it recorded the type of weapon that inflicted the "injury" and whether the person who was "hit" required a medic or needed a body bag. To make the engagement realistic, each weapon produced the same sound as firing live ordinance, unless a suppressor was used.

Tamala and three of his men got into position and took out the four perimeter guards before they knew what had happened. Now out of the exercise, the men picked a comfortable tree to sit and lean against as they watched all but two of the rescue team approach the shack. Those who stayed back provided overwatch, which meant taking a position to protect the others.

A breaching charge blew the front door off its hinges, and Nabar threw a stun grenade inside. This produced a blinding flash of light and a one hundred and seventy decibel sound—both of which temporarily disoriented an enemy's senses. As this was a standard breaching procedure, in anticipation of this, the "terrorist" team leader stationed the junior members of his unit inside the shack. Those more senior, who had been through this type of exercise, forwent the pleasure of having a headache and their ears ringing for the next hour.

The mission went flawlessly—the four terrorists inside surrendered, and they rescued the hostage. With the exercise over, the perimeter guards returned to the shack and retrieved their gear, while the lieutenant grabbed a backpack from the rear of the shack and brought it outside. Removing a black box and a small portable antenna, he connected the two and pushed the green button atop the battery-powered device. After adjusting the antenna to point towards a gap in the canopy cover, the lieutenant informed the base that the exercise was over, and both teams were proceeding to the extraction point. "Three hours until our taxi arrives," he said as he restowed the communications equipment. "Has anyone got an aspirin?"

Nabar took a plastic bottle from his backpack and threw it two him. The lieutenant dry-swallowed two and tossed the bottle back.

Tamala took the lead as they began their four-mile journey. There were fifteen men—Tamala's team, eight ex-terrorists, and the hostage. Thirty feet into it, four ex-terrorists and the hostage lay dead on the ground.

The speed of a missile fired from a drone varies according to the weapon system. However, a good rule of thumb is that it travels at approximately nine hundred and ninety-five mph, or Mach 1.3. On impact, a small missile has a kill radius of around fifteen feet and a wounding perimeter of sixty-five. Larger ones have four times that lethality and wounding radius. The missile that impacted the ground beside the lieutenant, killing him and four Kopassus soldiers, was small.

"Take cover," Tamala ordered following the explosion. Looking through the gap in the canopy, he heard and then saw a large drone pass overhead. It carried two weapons beneath each wing.

The "terrorist" team broke left while the "rescue" team ran straight ahead towards the jungle. They didn't coordinate that split, but that's what happened after the explosion—the teams instinctively sticking together as they dashed for cover.

"Someone should tell the brainiacs at HQ," Nabar said, speaking to the unit through his headset mic and pronouncing each letter separately, "that they're using live warheads."

Tamala was a few feet in front of Nabar when he suddenly stopped and waved the team ahead. Turning around, he saw the backpack containing the communications gear lying a few feet from the lieutenant's body. "Embed yourselves in the vegetation," he said into his mic. "I'm going back for the transceiver to tell ops to call off the attack; otherwise, none of us are making it out of here alive." Not waiting for a response, he ran in the opposite direction of the jungle undergrowth and into the open.

The "terrorist" team was the first to enter the jungle and quickly became invisible within the thick vegetation. Seconds later, a fireball exploded in their vicinity. Tamala did a roll call. Only his team responded.

"Ya Tuhan," Tamala said, which was the Indonesian equivalent of oh my God. "Spread out!" he commanded. "I'm thinking that drone has an infrared sensor that detects body heat." Tamala grabbed the backpack and, staying in the open because the only hole in the jungle canopy was above him, removed the transceiver and the dish antenna. He hoped the drone would take its time circling back because he needed to reach the operations center and call off the attack. If he couldn't, it was only a matter of time until they were all dead.

Connecting the antenna to the transceiver, he pointed it at the sky and pressed the green button. Seconds later, he was speaking to the Kopassus operations center. The conversation took a little more than a minute, after which he powered off the equipment, returned it to the backpack, slung it over his shoulder, and ran to where he saw his team enter the jungle.

"That's not our drone," Tamala said as he forced his way into the dense growth. They're sending an attack aircraft to take it out, but ops can't tell me when it'll arrive."

"What do you want to do?" Nabar asked.

"Get out of here. But the only patch of ground large enough for our transport to land is where we got off it. We can't go as a group. Each of us has to make our way separately. I counted four missiles on the drone. If we stay apart, they can't kill us all."

For the next three hours, they hacked their way through the jungle. It was eerily quiet as they closed in on the extraction site. Tamala wasn't sure whether the drone was in the area because he never heard it, and it was impossible to see an aircraft through the thick canopy cover. However, that question was answered several minutes later when he heard an explosion a third of a mile to his left, the detonation shaking the ground beneath his feet. Following a roll call, Nabar and Fanetri were the only members of his team to respond. Three didn't. He guessed they inadvertently got too close to one another without realizing it. "Keep moving," he ordered. "We're getting close."

Tamala arrived at the extraction site thirty minutes later and saw Nabar and Fanetri coming through the jungle twenty yards from him. The helicopter that operations promised was nowhere in sight. Instead, he saw the drone coming directly towards them. Since a missile traveled faster than the speed of sound, it was pointless to run. He wondered if he'd know the moment of his death or if it would just be lights out. That question was never answered because what happened next occurred in a flash. No sooner had he raised his middle finger in a last act of defiance, communicating to the drone operator he could put that where the sun didn't shine, than he saw the aircraft explode in a bright red and orange fireball.

"Sialan!" Tamala yelled, the Indonesian profanity covering the entire spectrum between WTF and son of a bitch. "I think the air force has arrived."

Jae-Hwa Ock stormed out of the Korean People's Air Force operations center in Pyongyang, leaving behind the stunned twenty-three-year-old pilot who'd flown the WZ-7 Soaring Dragon drone. The indicator panel in front of him was a sea of red lights, each indicating a malfunction on the aircraft. Additionally, the LED view screen, which carried real-time video imagery seconds before, and where he saw Tamala giving him the middle finger, went dark. Neither the pilot nor Ock knew what happened to this costly UAV they purchased from China. However, with every system having failed, there was no doubt it crashed and was now a pile of junk. Catastrophically, that junk was in another country. Ock, a realist, knew it wouldn't take long for Indonesian intelligence to piece together the wreckage and determine the type of drone and who owned it. The ownership was evident given that Kim Jong-un insisted on placing the North Korean flag on the fuselage and wings of every UAV. He considered arguing against it for the very reason of what just happened. Without markings, North Korea could point the finger at China, or another Asian country that purchased the same drone from them, and plausibly deny it was their aircraft. Who was to say it was North Korean? However, making suggestions that went counter to what the supreme leader wanted never worked well for the person expressing a countervailing point of view because they usually went missing shortly after expressing their opinion.

Ock walked down a dimly lit stark gray hallway until he was far enough away from the control room where no one could hear him. He then made the call that he dreaded, knowing that failure always annoyed the supreme leader to the point of anger. And Kim Jong-un, who could kill anyone without consequence, was not a person anyone wanted to anger.

The conversation went better than expected. That meant Ock wasn't going to die for telling his employer he'd lost the costly and difficult to obtain Soaring Dragon drone and couldn't confirm it took out its targets, Major Tamala and Captain Nabar. It would take a day to know if they were two of the three who survived.

"If they're alive, find another way to kill them and do it quickly. If there's another failure, my next conversation will be with your replacement," Kim Jong-un said before ending the call.

CHAPTER 3

Gunter Wayan and Eka Endah lived in a forty-eight thousand square feet mansion at the Bulgari resort in Bali. Wayan, who never had more than one client at a time and whose vehicle was perpetually on life support, wasn't wealthy. Their residence, which overlooked the Indian Ocean, was provided to them for life by the resort owner in gratitude for saving her life. The private investigator and his former assistant, an equal partner in W&E Investigations, recently began living together and used the mansion as their home and office.

Thirty-three years old and five feet seven inches tall, Wayan had black hair, brown eyes, and coffee brown skin. Eka, a statuesque brunette, was one inch shorter. She was twenty-six years old, had silken hair cascading over tawny brown shoulders, an athletic build, shapely legs, and ample breasts. Men did a double take whenever they saw her.

Formerly a detective with the police department in Bali, Wayan was technically fired for stealing five thousand dollars from a stack of two million following a raid on a drug dealer's home. Technically fired meant a friend negotiated his resignation instead of being tossed out. The former detective didn't take the money to embellish his lifestyle or pay for vices. Instead, he used it for cancer treatments for his wife after his insurance company denied coverage because they considered the medication experimental. In the end, what she received extended her life by a year.

After leaving the force, Wayan turned to the only skills he knew and started a private investigation agency. He expected his experience to drive clients to him and that he could get money from the bank to open an office. He learned this was not in sync with reality the day he went to the bank and was denied a loan after a five-minute conversation with the lending officer.

"Wayan, you're unemployed, have no significant assets, and no clients or potential clients. There's no way, at this moment, you can repay a loan."

The ex-detective, acknowledging the bank officer was right, left feeling he'd failed not only himself but also his late wife. Not one to give up, and wanting to prove the lending officer wrong, he dug in and worked relentlessly to establish a practice. However, he could never attract more than a single client at a time. The reason for this, he discovered after speaking to some who'd turned him down, was that he wasn't a large or established investigative agency. They didn't like going to a home office because it made them feel the person they were employing had fewer skills than those who worked in a large firm with a staff of minions. They reasoned that if he had the same expertise, why was he working from his apartment? Lastly, some prospective clients felt they couldn't trust him, given the rumors of why he left the police force. Therefore, without a retirement income or savings, he was dead broke and on financial life support as he tried to attract clients. Those he did sign couldn't afford the fees charged by mainstream firms and were barely better off than him.

The relationship between Wayan and Endah was complicated. Wayan was terrible at documentation, paying bills, and just about everything else except for investigative work. Eka was detail-oriented, and nothing escaped her. She began working for him when a friend told her a private investigator she knew was looking for someone to run his back office, although she didn't know if it was full or part-time because he was a sole practitioner. Eka was wealthy. However, she didn't feel good about living off her inheritance. Instead, she wanted to take a job and work for someone who helped others. That was important because her mother told her not long before her death that no matter how much wealth she accumulated, her life was a failure unless she helped those in need. Her mother volunteered at a local hospital and shelter. Eka wanted to take a different approach and was trying to determine what that would be when she interviewed with Wayan. In their meeting, she had a good feeling about him after listening to some of the investigations he'd undertaken and the effect it had on his client's life. She went with her gut and accepted the job. Although she was seldom paid on time, she came to respect his ethics, seeing he cared more about helping those in need than getting a fee. In her opinion, that made Wayan a terrible businessperson but a good human being. Respecting his propensity for helping those in distress, whether or not they had money, she continued to work for him because having a role in helping others made her feel good.

There was no romantic involvement before they moved into the mansion. Eka later learned that he'd kept his feelings for her in check and didn't pursue a relationship because he felt that would be not only disloyal to his late wife, who he still loved, but also unfair to Eka because of the torch he carried.

"That sounds like the act of a caring and thoughtful husband," Eka responded to him when she found out. "Don't ever stop loving her, and she'll never leave your heart."

Wayan took that advice, opened himself to a relationship with her, and took it one day at a time.

October 8, 2021

As was their routine, Wayan and Eka rose at seven-thirty a.m. and spent thirty minutes getting ready. Wayan entered the kitchen around eight a.m., went straight to the Keurig coffee maker, and prepared two cups of Lavazza Perfetto Espresso Roast coffee. Balancing a brimming cup in each hand, he carried them onto the back deck, where Eka sat at a patio table that looked out to the deep blue of the Indian Ocean. Neither had their iPhone or iPad. They used this time to relax and enjoy the view and each other's company. However, this routine took a sharp detour when someone pressed the doorbell. Wayan went to see who was there. Opening the door, he saw it was First Lieutenant Suton Persik.

"How did you know we'd be up? And why are you here?" Wayan asked in rapid succession, the smile on his face showing that he was happy to see him.

"In answer to your first question, you told me your routine. I find it enviable that you both can sleep so late. I'm paranoid by nature and don't sleep well. In answer to your second, I'll tell you once you put a high-octane coffee in my hands because I'm severely under-caffeinated."

"Fair enough," Wayan replied as he led him into the kitchen.

After preparing the coffee and handing it to him, they walked onto the patio. When Eka saw Persik, she got up and kissed him on the cheek. "And what brings you here at this hour?" she asked.

"Can't a friend just drop in for a cup of coffee?"

"You only visit when you have an agenda. You're one of the most straightforward people I know, which is one reason I like you," Wayan interjected.

"You're right. I'm here because I need a favor. I want you to investigate something and keep it low-key so that no one in the department will know."

"Is this personal?" Eka asked.

Persik shook his head in the negative. "I promised to help someone."

"What do they want you, or should I say us, to do?" Wayan asked.

"Investigate the circumstances preceding the murder of a farmer in Sumbawa. That area is outside my jurisdiction."

"Aren't the local police investigating?" Eka asked.

"Not what you'll be looking at."

"Why?"

"They refuse."

"They refuse to investigate a killing?"

"They're not refusing to investigate the murder. They're refusing to investigate the incident preceding it. I believe there's a connection."

"Start at the beginning," Wayan said.

After taking a sip of coffee, Persik began. "Three days ago, the military conducted a hostage rescue exercise in Sumbawa. There's a large military training area on the west end of the archipelago. As a policy, the government announces the date and time of all exercises in advance to alert civilian air traffic that military aircraft will be flying in the area at low levels. Have you ever been to Sumbawa?"

Wayan and Eka confessed they hadn't.

"Neither have I, even though it's only two hundred miles from Bali. I recently learned this archipelago encompasses an area of six thousand square miles and has a population of a million and a half people who primarily make their living in agriculture and the services associated with it."

"Not exactly a hot tourist destination," Wayan added.

"Far from it. Anyway, following a recent military exercise, the farmer who owns the property next to their landing zone filed a police complaint claiming a government aircraft crashed on his farm and started a fire that destroyed part of his sandalwood crops."

"The murdered farmer," Eka clarified.

"Yes."

"What do you want us to investigate?" Wayan asked.

"Verify the aircraft crash, for starters."

"There's nothing on social media or in the news about a crash."

"I think it was military. They don't like to admit to a crash because they believe it decreases the public's confidence in our armed forces."

"Were there bodies?"

Persik shrugged, indicating he didn't know.

"There are bound to be pieces of the aircraft on the farm,"

Wayan said. "They may have government markings or military spec numbers."

"This is where it gets complicated. The farmer told the police the military brought large trucks onto his property, loaded almost every scrap of the wreckage into them, and drove away without explanation."

"Almost every scarp?" Eka asked, picking up on the exclusion.

"I'll get to that. The farmer was pissed because he wanted reimbursement for his lost crops, and the government wouldn't return his calls. Therefore, he goes to the local police and files a complaint."

"Against the government? The police hate investigating the government," Wayan said. "It's like David taking on Goliath, except with a different outcome."

"That's the way it usually ends," Persik conceded. "The police told the farmer to be patient because it could take some time. The farmer sees the writing on the wall and knows his complaint isn't going anywhere. Angry, he finds the office of the department's captain and barges into it, telling him he needs to get off his ass or he's going to the local paper and name him as the bureaucrat who's holding things up."

"Shit flows downhill," Wayan said, accurately predicting what occurred next.

"You know it does. The captain pulls two officers off whatever they're doing and tells them to accompany the man to the farm and begin an investigation. When the officers get there, there's no wreckage. What the farmer points to as being the crash site is a scorched indentation in the ground. The officers are local, and they know holes like these are dug to burn plant debris after a harvest. With no evidence to substantiate the farmer's claim, they return to the station and file a report saying they saw no sign of a crash."

"But you believe the farmer, who's now dead, or you wouldn't be here," Eka stated. "Why?"

"As I said, I promised someone I'd investigate."

"Who?"

"The farmer's brother. My department can't become involved because the crash occurred in another jurisdiction, but you and Wayan can look into it."

"There wouldn't be bodies if it was a military drone," Eka said. "The government would want to keep its drone program under wraps."

"That's a good thought," Persik said. "Earlier, Eka questioned my use of the word almost. That's because the farmer hid a piece of the wreckage before going to the police."

"Why?"

"I don't know. It could be paranoia, protecting the evidence, or distrusting the government. Take your pick or add another reason."

"Did he show this wreckage to the two police officers?" Wayan asked.

"Yes. But they didn't believe him because there was no aircraft wreckage. They accused the farmer of fabricating what he showed, particularly because of the unusual marking on it."

"Which was?"

"A North Korean flag."

Wayan and Eka looked at him with an expression of surprise.

"That suggests a North Korean drone crashed in Sumbawa while observing a military exercise. Why would they care about the Indonesian military? Whatever the reason, it seems the government finds out about the crash, or shoots the drone down, and hauls whatever's left of the aircraft away. I understand why they want to keep this a secret. The international implications of a North Korean aircraft in our sovereign airspace are huge," Eka said. "They didn't want a farmer to expose the incident until the government decided how to confront North Korea."

"How did the farmer die?" Wayan asked.

"A burglar killed him."

"When?"

"The day after he filed the complaint."

"That's suspicious and convenient," Eka commented.

"Especially when a search of the property doesn't turn up the piece of wreckage he showed the officers," Persik added.

"Do you believe the government killed him?" Wayan asked.

"No, because his death invites an investigation. But someone wasn't thinking. If the government had him sign a non-disclosure and paid for his crops, everyone would have got what they wanted."

"Bureaucrats aren't linear thinkers. They ignored him," Wayan added.

"What's the name of the farmer and his brother who works at the department?" Eka asked.

"The farmer's name is Sehat Nabar. His brother is Timur—a senior lab tech in the department. He became frustrated with the lack of action by the Sumbawa police and asked if I could help."

"Any relation to Captain Bakti Nabar?" Wayan asked.

"His father."

Wayan and Eka expressed disbelief, which quickly transitioned to sadness.

"How's he taking it?" Eka asked.

"He feels guilty about not seeing his father when he cleared the jungle. However, the three team survivors were ordered to get on the evac helicopter and return to Jakarta immediately to be debriefed. Now, he wants answers, especially after learning of the police report his father filed and the piece of wreckage he showed the police. He doesn't believe his father died because of a robbery."

"Our investigation puts us on a collision course with the local police and the government. We could also attract the attention of North Korea. It could be a real shit show."

"Do whatever you have to do. I know you'll get answers. I'm not sure anyone else will."

"You'll get blowback from the local police. You may also get your hands slapped by the Ministry of Foreign Affairs and the Ministry of Defense."

"I won't. You will. They won't know I'm involved."

Wayan gave him an understanding nod. "I take it this investigation is pro bono?"

"I'll make it up to you."

"That's alright; I'm used to being poor."

"When can you get started?"

"As it happens, we have no schedule conflicts with our other clients."

"We don't have any other clients," Eka added.

"Then I guess we can begin now since we're at our usual starting point."

"Which is?" Persik asked.

"Having no leads or clues and trying to extract information from people who don't want to talk with us."

"At least, unlike your last case, no one will try to kill you," Persik said, not knowing how wrong that statement would be.

CHAPTER 4

October 9, 2021

Sapto Wirjawan was a human trafficker, smuggler, and profiteer. A nefarious private contractor, he had an international reputation with the underbelly of humanity for never failing to deliver on a contract. He limited his operation to Indonesia, which had seventeen thousand islands and two hundred seventy million people. He was the underworld's go-to contractor for illegal activities within the country, inheriting that distinction now that his previous competitor, Malam Dault, was dead.

The professional low-life was five feet, six inches tall, and was shockingly unattractive—having a face that only a mother could love. He was thirty four years old, bald, had pecan brown skin, hard brown eyes, and tipped the scale at two hundred fifty pounds. The scar on his left cheek, which required twelve stitches, came from a fight in his youth that ended with him killing the assailant with his knife after he'd broken the person's hand and taken the weapon from him.

He had three vices in which he overindulged—smoking, food, and alcohol. His teeth, fingertips, and nails were yellowed from smoking, and he was perpetually short of wind and stamina. The one thing he had going for him was that he was brilliant. Having an IQ of one hundred forty, he was statistically a genius.

He lived in Canggu, the same village in which he was born. The small coastal community on the south coast of Bali had three law enforcement officers—all on his payroll. Since his illicit activities were impossible to hide from locals, he addressed this issue with a combination of fear and generosity. The fear came from killing anyone who mentioned, for whatever reason, his activities. The generosity was that every household received a monthly stipend to mind their own business and develop amnesia if anyone asked about him. This combination worked well for the decade he'd operated his business.

Because Indonesia had thousands of islands, his illicit activities required a fast, low visibility vessel that could operate in all but the most extreme sea conditions. Therefore, he commissioned the construction of a VSV or very slender vessel. As wide as it was tall, this semi-submersible had a sharp bow that punched through the waves instead of riding on top of them, even in stormy seas. Because it was also extremely fast, it significantly lowered the exposure time at sea.

He kept the VSV at a pier deep inside a small inlet near his home. Carved out of the jungle by nature, the channel meandered for several dozen miles before ending at a wall of vegetation. With the triple canopy jungle cover prevalent throughout the area and extending over both sides of the narrow channel—the vessel, dock, and wooden support structures were impossible to see from the air.

Wirjawan's illegal activities made him an unconscionable amount of money. He used a stack of this cash to purchase the highest hill in the area, buying the homes of the hundred-plus families living there at prices that allowed them to construct other residences multiple times the size of their previous domicile. The twenty thousand square feet tri-level place he built looked more like a Four Seasons hotel than a home. The roof was constructed with Bangkirai wood, and the floors were Ujung Pandang stone. The furnishings used Suar wood, which some referred to as South American walnut, and were custom made to accommodate Wirjawan's out-of-proportion height and girth.

When Jae-Hwa Ock's airport taxi arrived at the residence at noon, he got out of the vehicle in front of the twin gates—adjoined at either end by the ten-foot stone wall that surrounded the hill. Pressing the button on the call box, he announced he wanted to negotiate a contract—the standard terminology for requesting an audience with Wirjawan. He would have liked to call the gangster and conduct their business over a secure line, but that couldn't happen because the obese profiteer didn't have a phone. He was distrustful of electronic devices, fearing they could provide a way for foreign and domestic police and intelligence agencies to discover his business activities and contacts. Twenty seconds after pressing the button, a voice dripping with arrogance told Ock to proceed to the residence.

When he arrived at the front door, a man in his twenties was waiting. He was tall, athletic, and dressed in khaki pants and a short-sleeved cotton Batik shirt in a blue leaf shadow pattern. Ock could see a bulge in the back of his shirt and at the bottom of his right pant leg, indicating he was carrying at least two weapons. The man asked for his passport, which the North Korean handed over. As he thumbed through it, Ock looked past the open front door and into the residence. Inside, he saw a tough-looking man pointing an Ingram Mac-11 subcompact submachine gun at him. After looking at the passport, the man put it in his pocket, expertly patted Ock down, and led him inside. The Ingram-carrying guard followed at a distance.

Wirjawan was sitting behind his office desk and didn't bother standing when the deputy head of the North Korean secret police entered. Instead, holding the stub of an unfiltered Kretek cigarette, a blend of tobacco, cloves, and other flavors, he pointed to the chair in front of him. Even though they'd done business before, the gangster never acknowledged their past relationship because he considered every contract one and done. The profiteer crushed the Kretek in his ashtray, which overflowed with the remnants of the three packs of cancer sticks he consumed each day, and extended an arm toward his guard. The person who'd greeted Ock removed the passport from his pocket and handed it to him, afterward retreating to the rear of the room where he stood to the left of the person carrying the Ingram.

"Who told you about me?" he asked in a gruff voice, after lighting another Kretek and taking a long pull.

The question caught the North Korean by surprise since they'd done business before. However, since he worked for a murderous psychopathic whack job, he wasn't intimated by these tactics and answered without objection. "General Min Kang made the introduction."

"I heard the general was caught stealing from your boss and suffered an especially gruesome death."

Ock didn't comment.

"What's your position in the government?"

He told him.

"And the contract?"

"Kidnap a man and a woman living in Bali and transport them to a cargo ship in international waters two hundred miles offshore." Ock removed three sheets of paper from his inside jacket pocket and handed them to him.

The obese criminal put out his cigarette and looked at the papers, which contained the names and photos of Wayan and Eka, along with where they lived and whatever else Ock's techs could get from the databases they hacked. "When?" Wirjawan asked.

"Tonight."

"The timing is tight."

"I have no alternative. They booked a flight to Sumbawa for early tomorrow afternoon, and I don't want them uncovering something there that must remain a private matter between governments. There are also several other issues at play—all of which are better left unexpressed."

"How did you find out they were going to the archipelago?" Wirjawan asked, suspicious of what he heard.

"My country is exceedingly good at manufacturing missiles, producing nuclear warheads, money-laundering, and hacking corporate and government computer systems. Not much else. Following an unforeseen incident in Sumbawa, we began monitoring police and government databases, airline manifests, and other informational sources to see what was known or suspected about the incident and if someone outside the local police force would be brought there to investigate what happened. Our monitoring discovered that a local farmer filed a complaint with the police, but I rectified that problem. Gunter Wayan and Eka Endah, whose names were already on our watch list for a different reason, were on a flight manifest. Ironically, I intended to come here tomorrow to ask you to kidnap them. Their involvement in Sumbawa accelerated my visit. What's your fee to kidnap and deliver them to the cargo ship?"

"Three million dollars."

Ock's eyes widened. "The last contract price was five hundred thousand dollars."

"I have no going rate. My fee is proportionate to the risk. You want me to kidnap these individuals within a matter of hours," Wirjawan said, tapping the three pages given him to make his point. "Gunter Wayan and Eka Endah aren't hapless civilians who can be taken lightly."

"I know nothing about them."

"You said they were on your watch list. Lie again, and I'll transport you to that ship in several boxes."

Sweat accumulated on Ock's forehead, and he broke off eye contact.

"They were responsible for the death of the head of another Indonesian crime family—someone who believed he was the predator and not the prey until they set their sights on him. As I said, the contract price is proportionate to the risks I take."

Ock, who wasn't about to return to North Korea without a contract, cleared his throat. "Three million dollars is acceptable."

"Wire it to this account," Wirjawan said, withdrawing a piece of paper from his desk and writing on it the name and address of an offshore bank, along with a string of numbers. "The money will need to arrive within the next three hours if I'm to meet your timeline."

Ock removed the satphone from his inside jacket pocket, extended the thick antenna, and made a call. He gave the information on the paper the gangster handed him to whoever he called and received the numerical confirmation number for the wire a minute later. He wrote it down and handed the paper back to Wirjawan.

"Three million dollars is in your account. The supreme leader wants them delivered to the ship unharmed. For both our sakes, make sure that happens."

October 10, 2021 @ 2 a.m.

It was a moonless night when the VSV anchored within sight of the jagged four hundred ninety-two-foot cliff in Uluwatu, Bali. Djoko Sueb, and the five members of his team, brought the raft from below deck and placed it in the tranquil water, securing it to the vessel while they retrieved the engine and batteries.

Sueb was five feet, nine inches tall, and was a muscular one hundred ninety-five pounds. He was thirty-two years old, had a deep and authoritative voice, short brown hair, deep brown eyes, and hickory-brown skin. His posture was ramrod straight, so much so that his subordinates joked he had a stick up his ass—although they weren't about to say this to his face for fear of having the crap beaten out of them.

Wirjawan referred to his hired thugs as a paramilitary unit because it sounded more foreboding than saying they were a mercenary security force. The only one of his thugs with military experience was Sueb, a former staff sergeant in the Indonesian army. He was a fanatic about training and ensured each of his men spent enough time at a makeshift gun range to qualify as an expert marksperson with both a handgun and a rifle. He also instituted a daily physical exercise regimen that was not unlike what he'd experienced in the army. Most of his men believed he missed the military and attempted to mold them into surrogate soldiers. Others thought he was a control freak who was afraid of being ill-prepared when confronting an adversary. Both beliefs were accurate. He missed the military and would have remained in it had they not thrown him out for relentlessly hazing the non-performer in his unit until he committed suicide in the barracks. The note he left behind said he couldn't take any more abuses from the staff sergeant and spelled out precisely what they were.

Sueb had fifteen men in his paramilitary unit, five of whom accompanied him on this mission. Their primary activity was kidnapping. Wirjawan needed to abduct ten children a week to satisfy the demand from his clients. While that number would raise significant concern in a small country, it was ignored in the world's fourth most populous nation. He didn't choose his victims at random. Their names and locations were provided by intermediaries, who received a commission to identify those who fit the profile they were given.

With the raft secure, two men brought the one hundred and ninety pounds Elco EP-50 electric motor from below deck and attached it to the raft's stern. Sueb and the others followed with four lithium-ion batteries, each weighing eighty-five pounds. Once connected to the motor and everyone was inside the raft, they cast off.

Sueb and his men wore sophisticated night-vision goggles that gave them exceptional visibility. Tonight, they needed these because, without a moon, the shore was otherwise impossible to see from the ocean's inky blackness. Twenty minutes after casting off from the VSV, the raft silently slid onto the narrow sand beach at the base of the cliff. Stepping onto the sand, the six men dragged the raft to a boulder and secured it.

Each thug carried a Pindad Senapan Serbu 1 assault rifle, called an SS1, and a Pindad G2 Combat Pistol. Both were manufactured in Indonesia and designed for tropical environments. Attached to their utility belt was an M-26c TASER, capable of hitting targets fifteen feet away. Powered by compressed nitrogen, it ejected two probes at one hundred eighty mph, which imparted a fifty thousand volt and twenty-six-watt charge. The result was an immediate loss of muscle and nerve control.

Sueb got detailed photos of the resort from online publicity photos and Google Earth. After studying these, he found a discreet way to enter the Bulgari resort—avoiding the razor-wire fence encircling the property, which had cameras atop many of its support posts. Guests were oblivious to the fence because of the sizeable distance between it and guest areas. He likewise avoided the main gate, which had retractable bollards across the entry and exit roads next to the guardhouse. Since the guards searched all entering vehicles, there wasn't a way to get weapons and equipment onto the property and make their escape without a major confrontation. That wasn't an option.

The solution to entering unseen came when he saw in the publicity photos a set of concrete stairs that paralleled the slant elevator and extended from the resort to the beach. There was no sign of security cameras along the stairway. Therefore, when the team stepped off the beach, they used the steep thirty-degree concrete stairway to penetrate the resort. Cognizant that they'd encounter security cameras once off the stairway, they stayed within the lush landscaping to remain hidden as they worked their way toward the mansion.

CHAPTER 5

The mansion in which Wayan and Eka lived had a very sophisticated alarm system. When triggered, it simultaneously sent intruder alerts to the Bulgari's security office and the Bali police. However, Wayan and Eka never set it when they went to bed. The reason was that, even though they were early risers, both were restless sleepers who habitually got up in the middle of the night to read or otherwise occupy themselves until starting to doze off—after which they returned to bed. In the mansion, this restlessness manifested itself with them going onto the pool deck and taking in the cool night air—cool having an entirely different meaning for Indonesians than those living north of the equator. Typically, they'd spend two hours outside before calling it a night and returning to their first-floor bedroom. Both were sound asleep when Sueb and his team arrived.

Sueb knew he'd encounter a sophisticated alarm system when he planned the home invasion because a residence of this size and value came with all the bells and whistles. Experience taught him the more wealth one obtained, the more security conscious they were. Consequently, he concluded there was no unobtrusive way to enter the mansion undetected because—once they picked the lock, opened the door, or broke a pane of glass, an alarm would sound. It was also reasonable to assume their targets had weapons given they were private investigators. He told his team this wouldn't be an easy snatch and dash, which was the norm for their kidnappings. Instead, things could get dicey.

He had a good idea of the interior. The layouts of four of the five resort mansions were on their website, each almost a cookie-cutter of the other. Speed was critical in any kidnapping. Because of the size of the residence, he divided his team. He and three men would go to the second floor, which had four bedrooms, while two searched the master suite.

The mansion's front door was seven feet high and made from teak. It was considered a western door because of its height. The typical Indonesian was highly superstitious, and their doors were small in width and height—the theory being that the smaller the space, the less chance an evil spirit could enter a domicile. Irrespective of the size of the door, the lock took forty seconds to pick, after which Sueb gently pushed it open. To everyone's surprise, no alarm sounded. However, the hinges, which last saw WD-40 the day they hung the door, emitted a low creaking sound. Sueb and his men cringed when they heard this. However, since there was nothing they could do, they quickly entered the residence and dispersed according to plan.

Tamala and Nabar, who were staying in adjacent rooms on the second floor, heard the creak and recognized the distinctive sound made by the front door. Wearing a t-shirt and boxer shorts, they left their rooms almost simultaneously and entered the hallway.

"I don't think that was Wayan or Eka. They told us they usually get up in the middle of the night and go on the patio. The front door is on the other side of the residence."

"It's not Persik," Tamala added, hearing snoring coming from his room. "Let's check this out and see if we have early morning visitors."

The mansion had night lights recessed in the ceiling. On timers, they provided enough visibility so that someone could walk around without crashing into something or stumbling on the stairs. When Tamala and Nabar went to the railing at the end of the hallway, they saw four men with automatic weapons heading for the staircase. The four were so focused on what was at eye level they didn't look up.

"I got this," Nabar whispered as he and Tamala retreated several feet and put their backs against the wall to avoid being seen.

As the first bad guy entered the hallway, the special forces captain grabbed the weapon out of his hands, executed a front snap kick, and sent him backward over the railing. While a fall from fifteen feet was survivable, the man had the misfortune of hitting his head on the foyer table—resulting in a cracked skull and death. The next bad guy, who was a couple of steps behind the first, didn't fare any better. Nabar, who had the first man's weapon, put a round into his head. After that, all hell broke loose.

When Sueb saw one of his team flying over the railing, followed by a gunshot, he unleashed a cascade of bullets at the top of the staircase and the hallway entrance. When the person next to him did the same, they slowly ascended the stairs in tandem.

Tamala and Nabar, who each held an assault rifle taken from an assailant, dove back onto the hallway floor and hunkered down as bullets slammed into the wall and ceiling in front of them.

Persik was now wide awake and ran into the hallway with his Pindad G2 handgun. Seeing Tamala and Nabar lying plat on in the hall, he decided that was a decidedly safer place to be.

"Any idea who's shooting at us?" Persik asked Tamala, who was to his right.

"None. They're not ex-military," he said, shouting to be heard over the echo of the gunfire throughout the mansion. "The way they approached and ascended the staircase tells me they're homegrown."

"Homegrown or not, they're carrying a lot of firepower."

Before Sueb and his team began destroying the second-floor hallway, the two men tasked with searching the master suite found Wayan and Eka asleep in bed. Removing their TASERs from their utility belts, each sent two probes into the person they were standing over. However, before they could relay this, Nabar put a bullet into one of the bad guys. When Sueb was told that Wayan and Eka were found and subdued, his focus shifted to keeping whoever was in the second-floor hallway pinned down while they were being taken to the raft.

"Get them to the raft," Sueb ordered, speaking into his mic. He told the person beside him to help.

Holding his position and periodically spraying bullets at the hallway entrance, Sueb watched as the three men dragged Wayan and Eka across the foyer. Once he heard they were on the beach, he let loose a final salvo and sprinted out the front door.

Tamala, Nabar, and Persik heard the scurry of footsteps across the foyer and, after waiting a few seconds, crawled to the end of the hallway and saw their assailants were gone.

"I'll call security and have them lock down the resort," Persik said.

"Give them a heads up these men have automatic weapons, and they won't come out ahead in a shootout if all they have are handguns. While you're at it, tell them not to shoot the two guys in their underwear who are carrying rifles."

Persik called resort security.

"I know where they're headed," Nabar told Tamala.

"You saw sand on their boots and the wet pant legs?"

Tamala confirmed he did.

"Let's get moving. We have a lot of ground to make up."

Barefoot, in their underwear, and carrying their assailant's assault rifles, they ran out of the mansion and, side by side, headed for the beach stairway. The two special forces officers didn't break a sweat as they weaved through the resort. When they got to the top of the stairway and looked down at the beach, they saw one of the kidnappers pointing a flashlight at the raft as the other lifted Wayan and Eka into it. Sueb had reached the beach and stepped into the raft. Since their rifles were fitted with night vision scopes, they considered taking a shot and dropping the bad guys. However, they held their fire for fear of hitting their friends because everyone was tightly packed within the raft, and it would only take a small gust of wind to put the bullet into the wrong person. Therefore, they watched as the raft entered the water and headed out to sea.

"They got away," Tamala said to Persik, who got dressed while they were gone.

Standing beside Persik were four police officers and three Bulgari security guards.

"I was telling everyone that you both were unarmed when you two took down these perps," Persik said, pointing to the bodies.

"Captain Nabar killed them," Tamala said.

"You both have brass balls," one officer commented.

"They still escaped. They had a raft at the edge of the water and were in it before we could stop them or get a clean shot."

"That means they're not going far," Persik said.

"I've ordered roadblocks for twenty miles in every direction," the police officer standing closest to Persik said. "I've also requested the KPLP to assist in the search. Now that you've told me about the raft, I'll update them." KPLP stood for Kesatuan Penjagaan Laut dan Pantai—Indonesia's sea and coast guard.

"They may try and hide in one of the inlets on this island," another officer added. "We'll get a helicopter in the air at daylight."

There was a knock at the front door. One officer opened it and let the police photographer, forensics tech, medical examiner, and coroner inside. After speaking with Persik, everyone spread out and got to work. Since the area where the two men were killed was relatively small, they finished three hours later and left, the police officers and Bulgari security departing the mansion with them.

"Any idea who was behind this kidnapping?" Tamala asked, throwing the question up for grabs.

"It could be someone who believes the occupants of this mansion are rich, and they can extract a huge ransom from family members,"

Nabar suggested. "It may not have been about Wayan and Eka at all."

"That's possible," Persik admitted. "However, since we aren't looking at human trafficking, because of the ages of those taken, and there are much easier ways to abduct trafficking victims than attacking a luxury resort, I believe they were after Wayan and Eka. If we identify the two Nabar killed, we have a clue who's behind it."

"Let me ask you a question," Tamala said. "If you needed to kidnap someone and wanted to hire the very best, who would you use?"

"Dault. However, since he's dead, I'd say Wirjawan because he's taken over Dault's business," Persik said, putting his hands in a steeple under his chin. "Thinking back to the last time we raided his house and searched the surrounding area, I recall he had a boat docked in a channel near his residence."

"They put Wayan and Eka into a raft," Tamala said.

"A raft isn't going to get them far. We might consider that they're being transferred to a boat."

"What type of boat did Wirjawan have in that channel?" Tamala asked.

"I know nothing about boats," Persik said, "It was long, skinny, and the top of it couldn't have been five feet above the water."

"Could it carry a raft?" Nabar asked.

"It's large enough."

"It's something to consider," Nabar added.

I'll have my office advise the KPLP about the vessel. I'm not sure they'll be able to do much when I tell them we think the raft might be rendezvous with a long, skinny boat somewhere in the Indian Ocean," Persik said with a look of dismay. "It would be like trying to find a pair of sunglasses dropped into the ocean."

"I might have a way to find those sunglasses," Tamala responded.

CHAPTER 6

Colonel Ganjar Durin was the military liaison for Indonesia's drone program. He was five feet, ten inches tall, weighed one hundred sixty pounds, had short salt and pepper hair, coffee-brown skin, and dark brown eyes. The twenty-two-year veteran was a distinguished pilot with an advanced degree in aeronautical engineering. He was currently in a hangar at the Halim Air Base in East Jakarta, looking at the wreckage recovered from a farm in Sumbawa. Technicians were painstakingly trying to reconstruct the UAV—the air-to-air missile reducing it to jagged pieces of metal. They'd pieced together enough to discern that it was a Chinese Soaring Dragon drone—an aircraft only manufactured in mainland China but sold to anyone with enough money to purchase it. With the flag of North Korea visible on the remnants of each wing, Durin had little doubt as to the owner of the scrap metal in front of him. Besides the wreckage, the unit he sent to the crash site recovered a rocket of North Korean manufacture, which miraculously hadn't exploded, further confirming who sent the aircraft.

The rocket indicated the drone's purpose because its weight severely limited the aircraft's range and loitering time. Therefore, it wasn't sent for reconnaissance but to carry out an attack. The question was: why send a drone three thousand miles, which was the distance between North Korea and Indonesia? That flight time dictated it needed to refuel coming and going. Also, why was a strike

43

ordered against those in an unclassified military exercise? The only conclusion he could draw was that North Korea, meaning Kim Jong-un since the country was a dictatorship, wanted to kill one or more of those involved in the exercise.

Durin pulled the records of those involved in the exercise, trying to determine who the North Koreas were after. He was going through the records for the third time when his cell phone chirped. It was Major Langit Tamala, who'd worked with him in determining the visual and thermal limitations of drones in a jungle environment. The major's ingenuity at hiding and making his team unobtrusive resulted in significant software modifications that enhanced the effectiveness of several drones.

Their conversation was brief. The major came straight to the point, telling the colonel about the kidnapping of Wayan and Eka and his belief that they were on a VSV that was going to transfer them to a larger boat. "I need your help to find them."

"Why should the military become involved?"

"The only way we're going to find the VSV is by using a drone."

"The KPLP is responsible for sea searches and interdictions involving civilians."

"A drone covers an infinitely wider area than a ship in a fraction of the time. Once they're transferred to another vessel, we'll never find them."

"Everything you've said is supposition. You don't know they're on a VSV and, if they are, that they're going to another ship. The only thing you know for sure is that someone kidnapped them."

Tamala admitted that was an accurate assessment.

Durin, who liked and respected the special forces officer, decided to give him the benefit of the doubt and bend the rules. "I'm about to test a new medium-altitude long-endurance drone, which we call MALE. It can stay in the air for twenty-four hours, has a service ceiling of thirty thousand feet, and a top speed of one hundred forty-six mph. The engineers configured its ViDAR to search a large area in a short amount of time." ViDAR was short for visual detection and ranging, picking up small objects that would otherwise go unnoticed by the drone operator.

"Finding the VSV would be a good way to test MALE's capabilities using ViDAR," Durin said. "The engineers will find the data useful. Text me photos of Wayan and Eka. I'll have them scanned into the drone's autonomous recognition system. Any idea of the vessel's direction? It's a big ocean."

"I'd say straight out to sea from the Bulgari and towards international waters. But that's Ouija board logic."

"Understood. I'll get back to you," Durin said and hung up.

The colonel was a get the job done and do the paperwork later type person and expected the same from his subordinates. He ordered the maintenance crew to tow the drone out of the hangar and prep it for launch. He then called the UAV pilot and told him to get behind his flight controls because he wanted the MALE airborne in less than fifteen minutes. Driving from the officer's quarters at seventy mph, he screeched to a stop in front of the operations building and ran inside. Fourteen minutes after the pilot received the call, the UAV roared down the runway.

"That looks like it," the drone pilot said to Durin, who was standing behind him. Both were looking at the video feed on the LED monitor.

"How far is it from shore?"

"One hundred and seventy-two miles."

"Speed?"

"Forty knots."

"Zoom in on the two standing on deck and run their images through the national database. Let's see if we get a facial recognition hit."

With a few clicks of his keyboard, the pilot input the images. Five minutes later, he received a response. Both men had long wrap sheets and were known to associate with Sapto Wirjawan.

"The range on a vessel that size and going that fast can't be over two hundred miles." Durin, who'd coordinated with the KPLP over the years and done his fair share of boating, was familiar with the operational capabilities of a wide variety of vessels. "It'll need to take on fuel to return to shore. Since the only filling station at sea is a ship, let's see who they're meeting."

The pilot continued to follow the VSV. Fifteen minutes later, it approached the Ja Ryu, a three hundred twenty-one feet long merchant ship at anchor that flew the North Korean flag. The VSV slowed and, coming alongside a gangway that extended from an open hatch near the bottom of the vessel to just above the water, secured the gangway to its deck.

"Tighten the focus on the screen to the VSV and merchant vessel instead of the wide-area view," Durin ordered.

The pilot did.

Unknown to Durin and the pilot, the name Ja Ryu was picked out of the air by the ship's captain and was the twelfth name given to this merchant vessel, its name and flag changing every so often to avoid the international sanctions placed on the rogue regime. In the following name change, it would become the Morning Sun.

Name changes were a common tactic for the North Korean merchant fleet, which numbered over one hundred twenty ships. The only weak link in this vessel's anonymity came from the captain's penchant for flying his country's flag at sea.

"A North Korean drone and now a North Korean vessel. This is getting interesting," Durin said. "I see two others came on the deck of the VSV. Zoom in on them."

The pilot adjusted the drone's camera.

"That's them," Durin exclaimed, seeing Wayan and Eka being escorted up the gangway and onto the Ja Ryu. As they watched, an alarm sounded, and the missile launch light on the pilot's console illuminated.

"Kotoran," the pilot screamed—the polite translation of which was *dirt*, as he instinctively put the drone into a steep descent. His reactions were fast but not quick enough. The missile clipped one of the MALE's wings and sent it somersaulting. Having lost control of the aircraft, the pilot helplessly watched as it twisted and turned until the LED monitor went dark on impact.

"Where did that missile come from?" Durin asked.

"The merchant ship. Missile detection and impact were too close together for it to come from another aircraft or vessel."

"Why does North Korea want these two so badly?" Durin asked himself as he phoned Tamala.

Following the call with Durin, Tamala walked into the kitchen, where Nabar and Persik were sitting at the counter having a cup of coffee. The look on his face told them something was wrong.

"The drone found the VSV and followed it to a merchant ship named the Ja Ryu, which was flying the North Korean flag. Wayan and Eka were transferred to that vessel," Tamala said.

"That's as bad as it gets," Persik added.

"Not quite. A missile took out the drone. That means we have no idea where the ship is or its course. Therefore, the KPLP can't rescue them. According to the colonel, if the captain of the Ja Ryu has any sense of survival, his vessel won't have the nautical tracking device that's standard on larger vessels."

"It's obvious, after what Wayan, Eka, and the two of you did to help Melis Woo destroy Kim Jong-un's money-laundering operation, where the ship is going," Persik said.

"We poked the bear, for sure. He's a vengeful and sadistic person. If we don't rescue them before that ship reaches North Korea, they'll be tortured to see if they know where Woo hid his money or how to find her," Tamala said. "After that, he'll execute them in a way we don't want to imagine."

"That explains why Wayan and Eka were kidnapped and not killed," Nabar added.

"I'd call their situation a dire emergency," Persik said.

Tamala and Nabar gave him a questioning look.

"Have you been asleep, Persik?" Nabar asked in an irritable and uncomprehending voice. "Of course, it's dire. They're on their way to North Korea and their death."

"I'm saying it's a dire emergency because Wayan gave me an encryption key and Melis Woo's email address. He said to contact her only in a dire emergency if he couldn't do it."

"Why would she help?" Nabar asked in a skeptical tone.

"We all know she has a soft spot for Wayan. He asked her to help Anna Bello, who would have spent the rest of her life in jail if it weren't for what she did," Persik answered.

"She got Anna's conviction overturned because she's an extraordinary computer hacker and got the evidence we needed to prove the judge was corrupt and the charges bogus. Penetrating a computer isn't the same as getting Wayan and Eka off a North Korean ship whose location is unknown. We'll need to use force to get them off that ship."

"Wayan said not to underestimate her. Judging from what she did for us, I'd say that's solid advice. What do we have to lose?"

Melis Woo's passport identified her as Abia Fares—a citizen of the United Arab Emirates who was born in Abu Dhabi. That was a lie. She was forty-three years old, born in Hong Kong, stood five foot, four inches tall, had black hair and light brown eyes and possessed a decent figure. The genius previously behind Kim Jong-un's global money-laundering mechanism, she set up his country's myriad of offshore bank accounts, dummy companies, and other ghost entities. These allowed North Korea and China to innocuously wash billions in hard currency and hide these funds offshore. A computer savant, she improved the hacking tools provided by these nation-states, bringing them to a new level which she shared with neither country.

She was well-compensated for her illegal activities and had a luxurious lifestyle until the day Gunter Wayan, Eka Endah, Langit Tamala, and Bakti Nabar barged into her Hong Kong office. Taking over the facility triggered a protocol set up by Woo's boss.

This dictated that a PLA hit team kills everyone in the money-laundering center—her included. Once the site was sterilized, the operation would recommence when a team from Beijing took over the following day. Woo knew about the protocol and that they had minutes to get out of the 101st-floor office before the hit team arrived. After convincing Wayan of the legitimacy of the hit, she made a deal with him. If he let her go, she'd get everyone safely out of Hong Kong. The former detective was good at judging people and believed her. They left a breath before the kill team arrived, escaping to Macau. While there, and before everyone went their separate ways, she relieved North Korea and Kim Jong-un of their wealth.

Unknown to *Forbes*, Abia Fares, AKA Melis Woo, was the eighth wealthiest woman in the world. Realizing the North Korean dictator would unrelentingly search the globe for her, she purchased a superyacht. Rechristening it the *Bolt Hole*, she sailed the world on the three hundred fifty million dollars, five hundred thirty-two feet long vessel with a crew of eighty-eight. No one, including Wayan, knew she lived on a boat. The only chink in her anonymity armor was that she'd developed a soft spot for Wayan. The reason for this was she liked his propensity for getting into trouble. The excitement and adrenalin rush of helping him escape whatever he'd gotten into was a stark contrast to her lavish but non-eventful life. Subsequently, she gave Wayan an email address and a series of one-time pads, or OTPs, which allowed them to communicate in an unbreakable code in the event of an emergency. Five minutes ago, she received an email from what should have been Wayan but instead was Suton Persik. It looked like he was in more trouble than usual.

Waiting on pins and needles—Persik, Tamala, and Nabar didn't know how long it would take Woo to respond to the email—if she ever would because her relationship was with Wayan and not Persik. Her reply came within an hour. To anyone who saw the encrypted message, it was gibberish until Persik took the OTP he'd been given and decrypted the mishmash of letters. *I'll help* was the incredibly brief response.

"She's short on details," Persik said.

"She's action-oriented and gives nothing away ahead of time," Tamala added, having a greater familiarity with Woo than Persik because he and Wayan were once tortured by her during an interrogation. "Whatever she's planning, Kim Jong-un will rue the day he kidnapped Wayan and Eka and made her angry."

"I hope that means he'll release them unharmed. I've dealt with enough psychopaths to know they're unpredictable. Woo still needs our help. We can start by finding the Ja Ryu for her."

"If the ship is going to Pyongyang, they won't want to waste time getting there. Therefore, let's assume their route will be a relatively straight course," Tamala said.

"Any ideas on how we find where the ship is on that line?" Persik asked.

"One, but I need to find something out first."

"Which is?"

"If Colonel Durin has a sense of humor."

CHAPTER 7

North Korea was under a microscope. An increasing number of its ships were intercepted by the United States thanks to sophisticated spy satellites that followed cargo from the manufacturing plant to the vessel and across the ocean. This resulted in the interdiction of the ship and confiscation of it and the cargo—putting a dent in North Korea's treasury.

Kim Jong-il, the predecessor miscreant to his slimeball son, Kim Jong-un, became increasingly frustrated with losing merchant vessels and the hard currency from their cargo. Subsequently, he ordered his staff to find an offshore site far from the homeland and the prying eyes of intelligence agencies and their satellites where they could conduct research and assemble weapons, including nuclear warheads, in absolute secrecy. A week later, his staff recommended Scops Island.

The North Korean dictator immediately liked the concept of a remote island facility. It was obvious he couldn't go to inspect it, not only because he was frail and the island wasn't exactly next door, or even in Asia, but because intelligence agencies constantly monitored his whereabouts. Instead, he sent his son and a team of experts on a ship carrying agricultural and fishery products to a country that western intelligence didn't give two flips about. The dictator believed American spy satellites would see the cargo and that the vessel was riding high—indicating what was onboard was light, the opposite of a shipment of missiles or arms.

When the ship arrived at Scops Island, geologists, contractors, engineers, and a dozen other specialties took measurements from the sophisticated instruments they brought ashore. They tested the maximum weight-bearing ability of the runway, collected soil samples, and assembled the technical data necessary to decide if it was feasible to construct the facility the supreme leader wanted. This process took two weeks. Once they departed, the team analyzed the data and wrote a detailed report of their findings so that it was ready to present to Kim Jong-il.

Presented by his son, the analysis concluded that construction of the complex was feasible but costly given the tremendous quantity of materials and equipment required and the lengthy transport to the site under extreme secrecy. It also noted that, since the underground facility would be significantly below the island's water table, constant pumping of the ever-encroaching water was required to prevent it from flooding. The dictator dismissed these concerns. His governing style was that if he decreed that something happen, it did. Therefore, he gave the order to move forward.

He knew he didn't have the money to construct the facility but believed he had a way to get it. Not wasting time, he contacted the president of Iran, Jadu Abdollahi, and deftly laid out his plan to construct a secret underground facility on an uninhabited island in the Arabian Sea. Since the island was not associated with either country, spies, electronic monitoring equipment, and increasingly sophisticated spy satellites would be absent. The dictator explained he intended to use the secrecy and closeness of the facility to Iran to produce its deadliest weapons for them. At the top of that list were nuclear warheads and medium and long-range missiles capable of carrying the MIRVs.

Abdollahi realized if their weapons came from the island, shipments to them would be faster, more reliable, and difficult to detect. Once he expressed these beliefs to Kim Jong-il, the dictator asked for the funding to construct the facility, admitting it was too early to calculate the ultimate cost. Knowing the value of the proposal, the Iranian president didn't blink. He approved construction financing and the purchase of a cargo ship, which they decided later would be berthed at the port of Mumbai to transport materials and equipment. Facility Number One became operational after one year of planning and two of construction, teams working 24/7 with an unrestricted budget. However, before construction was complete, Kim Jong-il died and was succeeded by his son.

The facility proved an immediate success. Able to operate without hiding what they produced or prototypes from intrusive satellite surveillance, it rapidly made and sent its new generation missiles to Iran. The first was the BM-25, which had a range of two thousand miles and could carry a nuclear warhead. This was groundbreaking because, for the first time, the Islamic State could launch a nuclear strike against cities as far away as Moscow. The Hwasong-16 followed in 2020. This two-stage monster was the world's largest liquid-fueled ICBM and carried four multiple independent reentry vehicles, or MIRVs, that could strike any city within the United States and Europe.

The president of Iran realized that, while the secrecy of Scops island was paramount, keeping the Hwasong-16 and the MIRVs a secret wasn't to his advantage. In negotiating with world powers, he needed leverage. Fear always worked. Knowing he could send a missile in their direction or at one of his adversaries, they'd be more amenable to negotiating. He let photos of the missile and MIRVs leak to several intelligence agencies. The result was nearly instantaneous. He found that, while the United States continued to tell him to twirl on it, European governments were open to purchasing oil and lowering the number of embargoed items. As trade increased, so did the money in the country's treasury. This allowed them to support more terrorist groups and threaten their neighbors with mass extinction at the press of a button. Israel was one of those countries.

However, producing missiles at Facility Number One had its challenges, the most significant of which was the inability to flight test prototypes before full-scale production for fear a satellite would detect the launch and the island's secrecy would be compromised. Therefore, they conducted the tests in North Korea. That necessitated disassembling the missile into small sections, crating them, shipping these to smaller North Korean ports, and trucking them to the appropriate manufacturing plant where they were assembled and sent to a test site for launch. This worked. As far as foreign intelligence agencies were concerned, the production and assembly facilities that produced these missiles were in North Korea.

For the next eight years, Facility Number One sent missiles to Iran under a veil of secrecy so absolute that no intelligence agency had an inkling of its existence. That changed on October 10, 2021, following an unexpected email to Kim Jong-un from Melis Woo.

Akbar Hassani was a major general in the Air Force of the Guardians of the Islamic Revolution, or AGIR, overseeing the operation and maintenance of his country's ballistic missiles. He was six feet, two inches tall, weighed one hundred eighty pounds, and had close-cropped hair, which was entirely gray and sparse near the back of his head. He had just finished giving the supreme leader of Iran and his advisors the plan they ordered him to prepare for the annihilation of Israel without Iran's fingerprints on the attack. In the age of technology, that wasn't a simple request because satellites monitored nearly every inch of their country and their neighbors. Additionally, the United States had labs that were so sophisticated they could determine the type of conventional explosive or nuclear material, who manufactured it, and the delivery vehicle. Knowing this sophistication, it took Hassani a year to put together an operation that satisfied the supreme leader's directive.

During his presentation, Hassani explained the difficulties they'd face. Israel possessed five layers of missile, rocket, and aircraft defenses. The first was David's Sling, which intercepted intermediate and long-range missiles in the terminal phase of flight. The second layer of protection was the Arrow II and III systems— exoatmospheric interceptors that targeted incoming missiles outside the earth's atmosphere. The third defensive layer was the Patriot system, which destroyed high-performance aircraft and intercepted medium and long-range tactical ballistic missiles. The fourth layer of defense was the Barak-8 weapons package—primarily employed against aircraft, helicopters, UAVs, and sea-skimming missiles. The fifth and final layer of protection Israel used was Iron Dome. Clustered around populated areas, it intercepted short-range rockets and artillery shells fired from a range of two and a half to forty miles.

The major general was uneasy because this was the first time anyone outside a small cadre of military planners knew the details of his plan, and he was wary a leak would destroy the operation. He was equally afraid of religious scholars and politicians. They knew little about strategic planning but had the authority to change the plan his staff had painstakingly put together unilaterally.

"And the equipment you're transporting by ship will neutralize the missile command and control sites?" the advisor seated to the right of the supreme leader asked. His question was in response to Hassani's statement that he would immobilize Israel's missile shields by generating a strong electromagnetic pulse, or EMP, that would destroy the electronics in the Israeli defense centers.

"Once the shields were down, our mathematicians calculated that the four MIRVs in each of the five Hwasong-16's have a ninety-nine percent probability of destroying their targets."

"Will the EMP devices be constructed here?" the same advisor asked.

"The design and construction will be in Tehran. We've calculated the individual pulse strengths needed for each of the five EMP devices and customized them to generate the required electromagnetic waves."

"And you're positive they won't trace this to us?"

Hassani explained the three ships transporting the devices

belong to a Liechtenstein company the Islamic State purchased through a series of dummy corporations. "The parts within the EMP devices are from Germany," he said. "None are of Middle Eastern manufacture."

The same advisor continued, asking how these devices would get past Israeli customs, which had a reputation for being sophisticated and wary of everything entering the country.

"The shipping company we purchased has a history of transporting equipment to Israel, which is why we bought it," Hassani stated. "Their three vessels have been offloading products in their port cities there for years. We didn't change the way the company operates. The ships have the same captains and crew and carry merchandise ordered by legitimate Israeli companies—as they always have. The only difference is they're transporting the EMP devices, which we hid inside generator casings. Each generator was ordered by a business we set up and control."

"And the crew knows nothing of this?" another advisor asked.

"They're in the dark."

Jadu Abdollahi raised his right hand slightly, indicating he wanted to speak. The room became quiet.

"How will you activate the EMP devices?"

"A communications device is connected to each. At the appropriate time, I'll make a group call and send a coded signal. This will initiate the triggers within the devices."

"And if customs or Israeli intelligence find them?"

"They will trace the generator orders to the Israeli companies owned by our agents. We funded the purchases of these businesses. However, our involvement was through a series of offshore corporations and banks and is undiscoverable."

"What about the agents?"

"Each has already volunteered to become a martyr. They know they'll die either from the detonation of the EMP device or the impact of the nuclear warhead. If discovered beforehand, they'll ingest a suicide pill. We've put online documentation showing they're part of a radical anti-Israeli neo-Nazi group in Germany that only has them as members. When the Israeli's investigate, they'll find this information. The German connection fits well given the parts used to construct the EMP devices."

Abdollahi nodded in satisfaction. "When will the ICBMs be delivered?"

"On October 18th—two days before launch."

"Five missiles sitting on an oil platform is hardly inconspicuous. That's a lengthy period of exposure."

"Each Hwasong-16 missile weighs one hundred twenty-one tons, has a length of eighty-two feet with the warhead atop it, and is eight feet in diameter," Hassani explained. "The transporter-erector-launcher, or TEL, that each sits on is slightly longer than the length of the missile and has eleven axles that support the weight. Although they're designed to transport, erect, and launch a missile, we'll be using them only as launch pads. These take time to be lifted by the platform crane from the ship's holds to the main deck. They're then positioned, leveled, and secured to the platform. Each missile then needs to be run through a battery of tests and fueled. Two days is cutting it close," Hassani countered.

Abdollahi again seemed satisfied with the answers. "The five cities remain as directed?" he asked.

"Jerusalem, Tel Aviv, Haifa, Ashdod, and Eilat," the major general confirmed. "They'll be reduced to ashes when the MIRVs destroy the military bases and command-and-control centers in those cities."

"What do our analysts believe will be the response from other countries, particularly the United States?"

"No one will know who to blame because the missiles didn't come from the homeland, which foreign military satellites will confirm. We'll be the logical suspect by default. However, other considerations will give us plausible deniability."

"Meaning?"

"Our Soumar cruise missile could hit any city in Israel. We

don't need to launch from outside our boundaries. An analysis of the nuclear residue will point to North Korea as the source of the U235. That regime has acknowledged nuclear warhead production and is known to sell weapons to the highest bidder."

"Then we'll proceed. In a little over two weeks, the Zionist state will cease to exist," the supreme leader said, the satisfaction of Israel's impending destruction reflected on the faces of everyone around him—except for Hassani. He'd been in the military long enough to know not to take anything for granted, recalling a Persian proverb he learned from his mother—*doubt is the key to knowledge.*

CHAPTER 8

October 10, 2021—Pyongyang, North Korea

Colonel Jae-haw Ock had just landed in Pyongyang on a Chinese commercial flight from Shanghai. Met in the terminal and escorted to a waiting car, he was told that the supreme leader wanted to see him in his underground office at his Ryongsong residence, thirteen miles from the airport. Traffic was light because most private citizens couldn't come close to affording a car. Those who could, worked either for the government or an industry essential to the nation's survival.

As he walked into Kim Jong-un's office, the dictator was in the middle of a tirade, slamming his right fist repeatedly on his desk. The subject of his ire, which Ock soon discovered, was the email from Melis Woo displayed on the dictator's computer.

"How is it," the dictator asked as he entered, "that your agents, and the scores of private investigators you hired, who searched every corner of the globe for her, failed to find a shred of a clue as to the whereabouts of Melis Woo? Yet, she's able to contact me." The dictator ranted that this was the western equivalent of rubbing egg in his face.

Ock wished his boss, the head of the secret service, was here to handle the situation. However, because he was old, ill, and hospitalized, which in North Korea meant he wasn't leaving in a vertical position, Ock was technically in charge. He read the email on the computer screen, quickly seeing what set off the supreme leader off were the demands made by Woo. He knew better than to say anything. He'd seen someone interrupt the dictator and offer his sympathy during a similar show of emotion. Seconds later, the dictator removed a gun from his desk drawer and emptied the fifteen-clip magazine into him—saying while discharging the weapon that he didn't want his sympathy. Word got around. After that, during one of his frequent rants, everyone in the room was afraid even to cough or clear their throat.

"Who does she think she is? No one gives me orders!" he shouted.

The e-mail ordered Kim Jong-un to take Gunter Wayan and Eka Endah unharmed at the nearest port or else. Woo, a stickler for detail, defined what she meant by *or else*. The dictator had twenty-four hours to release them, or she would reveal his activities on Scops Island to the world. He believed her.

Ock understood, and the supreme leader did as well, that even a rumor of what went on Scops Island would cause the United States and other countries to focus their surveillance and signals intelligence, or SIGINT, satellites on it. Once they did, Facility Number One was worthless. What further exacerbated his fury was that he was within a hair of shipping five Hwasong-16 missiles and launchers to the oil platform on the Hao Chang, which was docked at the facility. Behind it was the Abby Aurora, which was bringing a duplicate shipment to North Korea to increase his nation's strategic capabilities. Neither would arrive if she exposed the facility. Every vessel near the island would be stopped and boarded by American special forces or sent to the bottom of the ocean by a United States submarine in what later would be called a maritime mishap. Both vessels needed their cargo loaded and get away from the island as soon as possible to ensure they were undetected.

He knew Iran would destroy Israel with his warheads. That didn't bother him. What he did care about was keeping his largest customer happy by delivering what he promised—especially since the Chinese were getting increasingly close-fisted on funding his regime and purchasing his country's exports.

"Accelerate the loading and departure of both ships at the facility and tell them not to wait for the launch pads," Kim told Ock. "Divert the Ja Ryu to the platform and have the captain offload them there instead of at the facility."

"What about the private investigators?" he asked, hoping he didn't poke a hornet's nest.

"I'm not setting them free. I'm going to interrogate them to see what they know about that bitch's whereabouts and where she hid my money. Then, I'm going to kill them," Kim Jong-un responded. "Until then, they're my leverage to make sure Woo doesn't tell anyone about Facility Number One or disclose anything else she knows. Send a response to the email address she gave me. Tell her if she tells anyone about Scops Island, I'll execute her friends in a particularly gruesome manner."

"The Iranians may not have the platform ready if our ship leaves early. They're still preparing it."

"That's their problem. Our agreement is that I receive payment once the Hwasong-16's and their launchers arrive there. Call Major General Hassani and tell him that the shipment will get to the platform early. Don't explain why. We'll give him the expected arrival time later."

Kim Jong-un had several assistants whose job descriptions were better suited to accomplish what he'd ordered the deputy head of the secret police to do. One even spoke Arabic. However, neither Ock nor those assistants were brave enough to point that out to the dictator.

Ock phoned Hassani. The general wasn't thrilled because his platform crew was already working 24/7 and would be under even more pressure with the expedited arrival. However, knowing he didn't have a choice and that the supreme leader's advisors were looking up his ass and micro-evaluating everything he was doing, he asked for the ship's arrival times and said the platform would be ready. Ock followed the call to Hassani by sending Kim Jong-Un's response to Melis Woo's email, telling her to keep quiet or her friends would die. He didn't always agree with the dictator's actions, although he would never say that to anyone. He did in this situation because they needed to keep the island a secret, and he was losing confidence daily that his agents and the investigators he'd hired could find her. Unless he found Woo, he'd eventually be thrown under the bus, and someone else would take his place. Therefore, interrogating the private investigators might be the only way to get the answers he needed to stay alive.

After replying to the email, both Ock and Kim Jong-un believed they'd settled the matter, and Woo would have to accept it was their way or the highway. They were wrong. When her response came, it wasn't remotely what they expected—or wanted.

Colonel Durin didn't have much of a sense of humor under the best of circumstances. At this moment, the pendulum of levity was stuck in the opposite position the major needed for Durin to pat him on the back and say they should give it another shot. Therefore, the colonel refused when Tamala asked for another drone to find the Ja Ryu.

"I already had to explain how the military's newest drone was destroyed in a test flight that was supposed to be benign— meaning everyone involved, from the pilot to the maintenance crew, were familiarizing themselves with its operational capabilities. Familiarization flights aren't supposed to put the aircraft at the bottom of the ocean," he said. "The destruction of a second drone under similar circumstances would be career-ending."

Tamala understood that, in the military, accountability went with the job. Someone was always held responsible when something didn't go according to plan, and that person was usually the one in command. From there, shit rolled downhill to those of lower rank who were involved.

Once Durin vented, he lowered his intenseness a level or two. "To be honest, I'd like to send another drone, only this one won't be a wallflower," the colonel said, meaning it wouldn't be unarmed like its predecessor. "This one will have a rocket-carrying Type A personality. However, as much as I ache for that to happen, we can't endanger the lives of the hostages by sinking the vessel. I'll give you another drone. When we find the ship, and we will find it, we'll give the coordinates to the KPLP and have them interdict it, rescue the hostages, and throw the kidnappers into prison."

Tamala was at a loss for words, expecting Durin to maintain his refusal.

"I have a ScanEagle drone in the hangar," the colonel continued. "It has a loiter time of around twenty hours and can search a wide patch of ocean. I'll have it ready for flight in less than ten minutes. Since we know where the Ja Ryu shot down the MALE drone, and that ship isn't a speed demon, we'll have a good shot of finding it."

"How are you going to keep it from getting shot down?" Tamala asked.

"I have two hundred plus miles before the ScanEagle reaches the search area to figure that out. Let's hope I do," Durin said before ending the call.

The Ja Ryu was under the command of Captain Jae Cheup. He was forty-six years old, five feet, five inches tall, husky, and had black hair. At sea since the age of twelve, when he crewed for his father, who was the captain of another North Korea rust bucket, he'd been involved in a constant string of illegal maritime activities on behalf of his country.

His initial orders were to proceed to Facility Number One and deliver five Hwasong-16 TELs, which he'd off-load onto the Hao Chang. However, those orders changed when he received an encrypted call from Jae-Hwa Ock, diverting his vessel to within spitting distance of Indonesian waters. Once there, he was to rendezvous with a VSV and take on board two hostages, ensuring they remained healthy while keeping them locked in a compartment and under guard until his ship's return to Pyongyang. He followed those orders and, once they were aboard, again set course for Facility Number One. However, he didn't get far before he received another call from Ock, this one diverting him to an oil platform at a set of coordinates in the Arabian Sea. Upon receiving these orders, he changed the name of his vessel to the Morning Sun, the next name on the list he was given.

Cheup had no illusion that his orders came from Kim Jong-un even though Ock was the deputy head of the secret police. Subsequently, when they told him to take good care of the hostages, this meant his well-being was tied to their health and safety. He brought them on deck twice a day to get sun, fresh air, and exercise. He also made sure they ate well—receiving the same meals he was served. Because of this paranoia, when his ship's radar detected a drone shadowing the vessel, he was afraid it might have photographed his newly arrived passengers and would track the Ja Ryu until the Indonesian navy intercepted it. Knowing Kim Jong-un's way of dealing with those who failed him, he made a spur-of-the-moment decision and ordered one of his men to destroy the drone using a Stinger, an infrared surface-to-air missile. Once they obliterated the aircraft, he told the ship's engineer to give him flank speed so that the vessel could become an innocuous speck on the ocean.

After his call with Tamala, Durin sat down and analyzed the digital images from the now submerged scrap metal that was once the MALE drone. He focused on the crewman holding a shoulder-fired portable missile launcher, zooming in on the weapon. The enlarged image identified it as an FIM-92, referred to as a Stinger missile—an extraordinarily lethal fire and forget weapon that destroyed anything that came into its playground. However, that playground had limits—a range of five miles and an altitude below eleven thousand feet. Now that he knew what he was up against, he'd keep the ScanEagle outside those boundaries.

The pilot of the ScanEagle was an experienced drone operator who'd chased his fair share of vessels. From experience, he knew other captains increased the ship's speed to the maximum when fleeing an area after doing something illicit. They also maintained a straight course to get as far away as possible in the shortest amount of time. Cheup wasn't the exception. The drone's pilot found the Morning Sun, which he determined to be the Ja Ryu after looking at its photo and seeing that every feature, except for the name, matched. Several minutes after discovering the vessel, he saw on his LCD screen a crewman racing from below deck and pointing a missile launcher in his direction. However, the missile never left the launcher.

"Not getting a lock?" the pilot asked the crewman, knowing it was a one-way conversation. "The Stinger has a range of five miles. I'm two miles beyond that."

Durin was standing behind the pilot. "That looks like Wayan and Endah," he said, pointing to the man and woman at the bow of the ship. Beside them were two men with AK-47's.

The pilot zoomed in and confirmed their identity.

Durin felt he now had the evidence he needed to prove North Korea abducted two Indonesian citizens and held against their will on the same merchant vessel which downed the MALE drone over international waters. He attached an explanatory email to the drone's video and sent it to the defense minister, indicating he needed an expedited decision on how he wanted the ship intercepted. Because of the international implications, the minister reacted as if the email was nuclear waste. He kicked the can down the road to the president. Since bravery in politics is an oxymoron, the president sternly reminded him that Indonesia was only one of twenty-four countries with embassies in Pyongyang. He wasn't going to blow up this relationship by making a knee-jerk decision to attack a North Korean merchant vessel in international waters, even though it shot down one of his country's drones and appeared to kidnap two of its citizens. Therefore, the president did what most politicians do. He didn't say yes or no. Instead, he said he needed more facts before deciding on a course of action. In politispeak, that meant putting the decision-making process into a circular bureaucratic loop—the black hole of politics where anything sucked into it was never seen or heard of again.

CHAPTER 9

The National Reconnaissance Office, or NRO in Washington-speak, is the US government agency charged with designing, building, launching, and maintaining satellites for the intelligence community and the Department of Defense. Satellites are placed into a specific orbit depending on their function. A geosynchronous orbit enables a satellite to remain over one particular spot on the earth, generally at an altitude of twenty-two thousand miles, to keep an area under constant surveillance. Satellites placed in this orbit intercept electronic signals and communications. High-resolution images are taken from much lower orbits. Therefore, reconnaissance satellites such as the Keyhole series, abbreviated as KH, circle the globe every one hundred minutes or so at an altitude between one hundred seventy and six hundred twenty miles.

The KH-11 is a two-billion-dollar monster that's sometimes referred to as Kennen—for reasons known only to the government. The size of the Hubble Space Telescope, it weighs forty thousand pounds and measures sixty-five feet in length and ten feet in width. Lightweight and optically superior to the Hubble, its telescope is almost eight feet in diameter. This enables it to discern objects that are slightly smaller than four inches across as it orbits two hundred miles above the earth and races across the sky at eighteen thousand mph. Its cousin, the higher-orbiting Mentor—is a SIGINT satellite. It collects electronic and communications intelligence, respectively referred to as ELINT and COMINT. The Mentor weighs eleven thousand pounds and has an antenna three hundred thirty feet in diameter. The NSA has an undisclosed number of other satellites in orbit. These, along with aircraft, marine, and land-based listening posts, monitor devices that transmit an electronic signal—such as cell phones, radar systems, and so forth. If an electronic device sends a signal through the air, the NSA has recorded, analyzed, and stored it within its massive databases.

Captured data is first relayed to the Aerospace Data Facility at Buckley Air Force Base in Colorado, where eight hundred fifty NSA employees oversee the receipt and routing of the information. These intercepts then go to a specific center, depending on where they originated. Data from North Africa and particular areas in Europe and the Middle East go to a four thousand person, six hundred four thousand square feet building at Fort Gordon in Agusta, Georgia. If the intercepts are from Latin America and the rest of the Middle East and Europe, they're routed to the NSA's two thousand person facility in Lackland, Texas. A two hundred fifty thousand square feet, two thousand seven hundred employee facility in Oahu, Hawaii, focuses on Asian intercepts.

Not all NSA facilities are within the United States. Undisclosed overseas locations tap into the telecom switches of many countries, allowing them to record data and voice communications. Although the NSA is prohibited from spying on Americans, that prohibition has long ago gone by the wayside as it has over twenty listening posts that tap into US telecom switches.

The central repository for all this data is the Utah Data Center or UDC. Because of the massive amount of information the NSA collects and stores, the UDC was designed to handle yottabytes of data—a yottabyte is a septillion bytes or 500 quintillions (500,000,000,000,000,000,000) pages of text. The one million square foot digital storage facility in Bluffdale, Utah, which cost two billion dollars, is also tasked with decrypting conversations that nation-states and others believe to be unbreakable.

The last step in NSA's data collection and decryption process is an analysis by supercomputers. These search for telltale patterns which, if found, are flagged for review by an analyst. The person in charge of the agency's analytical functions is Libby Parra.

October 11, 2021—Fort Meade, Maryland

Within the agency, Libby Parra was a living legend. The consensus among her peers, and the bureaucrats who took credit for her work, was that she was the most intuitive and acute analyst who had ever worked at the NSA. The forty-six-year-old statuesque blonde, who'd kept her beauty with age, had never been married. Before being promoted to Chief, Global Issues Analysis Office, she spent twenty-eight years focusing on Russian intercepts. She was offered her current position five times, constantly turning it down because she understood the Russian mentality so precisely that she could predict what they would do with the same accuracy as if handed notes from their staff meetings. Although she'd put in enough time to call it a day and retire, she informed the commanding four-star general she was committed to working at the agency until she dropped at her desk. The reason for this, which she'd never explained to her colleagues or friends because it was personal and none of their business, was that she felt what she did would make America safer.

The current director, General Parker McInnes, took a different approach than his predecessors in getting her to join him at NSA headquarters at Fort Meade. While they touted increased pay, retirement benefits, and enhanced job stature, he convinced her the impact she would have on national security would be far more significant if she oversaw the agency's global analysis efforts. Therefore, America would be safer. That approach clicked, and she left her office at Fort Gordon in Georgia and moved to Maryland.

Alan Refkin

Currently, she was analyzing three ELINT intercepts flagged by an algorithm she'd designed. The set of rules in it focused on Kim Jong-un—who was of particular concern to the Oval Office, the NSA, and the National Command Authority, or NCA as it was referred to in the alphabet-driven lexicon of Washington.

The first intercept was an email to Kim Jong-un from a masked server. Whoever sent it was extremely good at their tradecraft, and neither she nor the agency techs could determine the identity or location of the sender. What set this email apart was that, unlike the others he received, the sender ordered the murderous dictator to do something. In this case, release Gunter Wayan and Eka Endah. They also warned that nonaction would result in the revelation of his country's activities on Scops Island.

Who's crazy enough to threaten Kim Jong-un? Who are Wayan and Endah? And where the hell is Scops Island? Parra asked herself in rapid succession.

Accessing the NSA database, she discovered Wayan was a disgraced Indonesian private investigator and Endah was his partner, both sharing a residence in Bali. She returned to the database and broadened her search to include all agency intercepts that mentioned their names in the past week. The results appeared on her screen less than a minute later after being routed through a translation program. Intercepts included conversations between Major Langit Tamala and Colonel Ganjar Durin, discussions between the minister of defense and the president of Indonesia, and so on. Parra next retrieved background information on Tamala, Durin, and others with whom she was not familiar. Putting everything together, she understood the how of Wayan and Endah's kidnapping and that Kim Jong-un was behind it—although the reason why remained a mystery.

Turning her attention to Scops Island, she discovered it was a patch of jungle eight hundred miles off the coast of Mumbai, India, and was once the site of a British prison. In the late 90s, it was purchased by a tech billionaire who was later forced to sell it to an offshore corporation during the world financial crisis. The map on an adjacent LED monitor showed it was in the middle of nowhere. The agency had virtually no data on it because it didn't come up in conversations with those hostile to the United States or its allies. Subsequently, it never warranted electronic or visual surveillance. That was about to change in a big way.

As Parra dug deeper, she retrieved the last week's intercepts from the Mentor satellite positioned over North Korea. Although these voice and data transmissions were encrypted, the cryptoanalysis supercomputers at the UDC defeated it. As she began reading, three caught her attention. The first was a conversation between Dae Cheup and Jae-Hwa Ock, the deputy head of the secret police, who was a known confidant of Kim Jong-un. She was familiar with Ock but not Cheup. It took fifteen minutes of delving into various databases to discover he was the captain of a North Korean merchant vessel.

Ock ordered Cheup to divert his vessel to a point just outside Indonesian waters, rendezvous with a small vessel, and bring on board two persons. Once they were on the ship, he could continue to Facility Number One.

The second intercept sent her pulse racing, with Ock instructing the person who answered his call to load five Hwasong-16 missiles and warheads onto the cargo ship ASAP and not wait for the launch pads to arrive. Once secured, the ship's captain would depart the island for the platform without delay.

Parra didn't know where the ship was or where it was going. North Korea routinely sold arms to anyone who had the money to pay the cash-starved regime. What made this shipment unusual was that it was transporting North Korea's largest ICBM. She believed Iran was the most likely buyer since they had the Hwasong-15 in their inventory. It made sense for them to upgrade to the newest missile. According to US intelligence, it had the flexibility to carry either a large conventional warhead or a MIRV with four nuclear warheads.

The third intercept was a second conversation between Ock and Cheup, this one changing the captain's destination from the island, as they called it, to a platform at a set of coordinates near Socotra Island, where he was to offload the missile launch pads. Since the call about the Hwasong-16's also mentioned the platform, Parra now knew the destination of the ICBMs and their launch pads.

Parra was frustrated she hadn't seen these intercepts sooner. Time was critical when acting on intelligence. However, she couldn't blame anyone. The supercomputer's programming automatically translated and routed the three intercepts to the North Korea section for review and analysis. However, since the intercepts only occurred a short time ago, she understood the analysts hadn't yet wrapped their arms around the context of the information—which is why they hadn't brought them to her attention.

She knew she couldn't read every satellite, aerial, marine, and ground-based intercept for governments and groups hostile to the United States. If there were two or three times the hours in a day, it still wouldn't be sufficient. Therefore, she prioritized her notifications by having algorithms that harvested, from the immense amount of data collected, intercepts that reflected her most immediate concerns. This didn't take analysts out of the picture. They still received the information; only she got it in parallel. Kim Jong-un, a first-class nut-job, was at the top of her special attention list because he could launch a nuclear weapon at a United States territory and threatened to do so in the past. However, now that she saw these intercepts, she needed to add an algorithm for Ock.

Is Facility Number One, Scops Island? Parra asked herself. *I'm betting it is because the missile launch pads were initially going to an island, the same word Ock used when describing the location of the Hwasong-16's that were to be loaded ASAP onto a cargo ship. Why bring ICBMs into the Arabian Sea? I think I know the answer.*

Parra pulled up the KH-11 reconnaissance photos for Iran, which she'd looked at an hour earlier. These captured Major General Akbar Hassani and the supreme leader's closest advisors at the House of Leadership in central Tehran, the supreme leader's residence, bureaucratic office, and principal workplace. Hassani was with this group on January 8, 2020—shortly before Iran launched its ballistic missiles at the Ayn al-Asad airbase in western Iraq and another airbase in Erbil. Both attacks were in response to the killing of Major General Qasem Soleimani by a United States drone. Given this meeting and the shipment of missiles and launch pads to the platform, she believed Iran was preparing for a more significant missile attack, this one possibly using nuclear warheads. It didn't take a mind reader to figure out their target or from where the attack would come. Para took what she had to McInnes.

"Based on the intercepts, it's probable Scops Island is a North Korea missile manufacturing facility which may also be constructing nuclear warheads," the director of the NSA said. "That they're transporting the missiles and launch pads to an Arabian Sea platform indicates there's a high likelihood they're preparing to launch the ICBMs at Israel, later denying their involvement because the missiles didn't come from their homeland."

"That's my thinking," Parra said.

"The question is: are we talking conventional or nuclear weapons? I want something less circumstantial before I present this to the NCA. Let's get eyes and ears on Scops Island, that platform, and shipping in the area."

"I'm on it."

"Nice work, Libby," McInnes said as she was leaving his office.

"Thank you, but collecting, analyzing, and acting on intercepts is a team effort."

"You'll never be a bureaucrat."

"From your lips to God's ears."

Once she left, McInnes called Abe Talman, the director of Mossad—the Israeli agency charged with obtaining foreign intelligence and foiling attacks. The agency's full name was Mossad Merkazi le-Modiin ule-Tafkidim Meyuhadim, which in Hebrew translated to Central Institute for Intelligence and Special Operations. It was one of three major intelligence organizations in Israel, the other two being Aman, which was military intelligence, and Shin Bet, which was the country's internal security service.

McInnes and Talman worked together in the past, preventing terrorist attacks in both nations. Although Mossad lacked the reconnaissance and SIGINT capabilities of the United States, it had far superior HUMINT or human intelligence. They embedded agents in sensitive positions within many governments which the United States couldn't penetrate.

The NSA director gave chapter and verse on what he knew, withholding the exact location of the platform because he didn't want Talman to attack it just yet. He also didn't provide recon photos of the gathering in Tehran because he didn't want the Israeli spymaster to know the upgraded photographic capabilities within the newest keyhole satellites. Since he didn't have time to order the photographs to be made less discernable, Talman would have to take his word and run with it.

"The Iranians know if they launched a strike against us, we would respond with a crippling retaliatory strike," Talman said.

"Not if they make a preemptive nuclear attack against those strategic capabilities."

"We have a very robust missile defense which will destroy warheads long before impact."

"Theoretically," McInnes, familiar with the Israeli defense system, interjected. "It's untested against this type of attack. Do you want to roll the dice?"

"No," Talman admitted, his voice revealing that he was reluctant to admit the missile defense shield wasn't perfect. "Give me the location of the platform and ships, and I'll destroy them. No one will learn this information came from your government."

"It's too soon to attack the platform. The missiles and probably the warheads are in transit. If you pull the trigger, the ships will divert and offload them at another location. If that happens, it's only a matter of time until you get a chance to test the missile defense system you're so proud of."

"Point taken."

CHAPTER 10

October 12, 2021—onboard the Ja Ryu

Gunter Wayan and Eka Endah were in a small compartment on the lower deck of the Ja Ryu, their accommodations a steel cube measuring ten feet by eight. There was a copious amount of rust on its bulkheads, and black mold covered the single air vent. As one entered, a bunk bed was to the right and a tiny table and two small chairs to the left. The mattresses, sheets, and blankets reeked of sweat and other bodily odors from the two crewmembers who Cheup kicked out to make room for his prisoners. The rest of the cabin was just as filthy, littered with empty water bottles, trash, and other debris tossed on the floor by the previous occupants.

Because the private investigators were kidnapped while in bed, they weren't wearing much when they came aboard the Ja Ryu. Eka was wearing a nightshirt—Wayan boxer shorts and a t-shirt. Since the merchant vessel didn't have spare clothing, Cheup gave each a pair of overalls and boots that he took from the lockers of crewmembers who were approximately their size. The bad news was that the garments had the same level of cleanliness and odor as their accommodations. The good was that it kept them warm in the dank confines of their steel compartment.

The captain stationed two guards outside their door and another at the end of the passageway. After the incident with the MALE drone, he stepped up security by adding a guard on their deck—this one stationed at the up ladder. Wayan and Eka could only leave their compartment to go to the communal bathroom at the end of the passageway, with only one allowed inside at a time. They were taken on deck twice a day, at no specific times, to get fresh air—the two guards outside their door serving as escorts.

When they returned from above deck, and the guards closed the door to their cabin, they sat on the edge of the bottom bunk, which was the most comfortable place to sit. Wayan leaned towards Eka, keeping his voice low so the guards outside their compartment couldn't listen to what he was about to say. "From hearing the crew speak Korean and seeing the North Korean flag on the stern, we knew from the moment we stepped onto this ship that Kim Jong-un had us kidnapped. I've done a fair amount of boating and, from the direction of the sun, I'm certain we're going northwest. That takes us deeper into the Indian Ocean. North Korea is directly north, towards the Yellow Sea. Wherever they're taking us, it's not there."

"Maybe this ship has a stop to make before then," Eka responded.

"You're probably right. It will be interesting to see where that is."

"And why that's a priority over getting us to North Korea so we can be asked where Melis Woo is and where she's hiding his money," Eka added.

"I might substitute the word torture for ask. There's no way we're walking away from this."

Eka agreed their future looked bleak. "Going back to the aircraft that was shot down, someone must know we're on this vessel and be tracking this ship. Otherwise, the captain wouldn't risk destroying it.

"We know it couldn't have been civilian—that would put a global spotlight on this ship and North Korea. I'm inclined to think it was a military drone or aircraft. However, that runs contrary to my belief that our government isn't willing to piss off Kim Jong-un to rescue two nobodies from a North Korean vessel in international waters. Indonesia will never stand up to him. That relationship outweighs our importance. Instead, the path of least resistance is for the governments to discuss the matter. North Korea will deny everything, even if the aircraft took photos of us on the deck of this ship. Therefore, wanting to avoid a confrontation and the risk of severing relations, both sides will forget about what occurred. Again, we're nobodies in this equation. If we want to escape and come out of this alive, it's up to us."

"I counted four guards—two are outside this compartment, and one is at the end of the passageway, and one beside the ladder leading to the deck above," Eka said. "Any ideas on how two unarmed captives overpower them and escape?"

"Yes, on overpowering the guards, but iffy to exceptionally iffy on the escape," Wayan answered.

"Explain the iffy to exceptionally iffy part."

"We need to come within sight of land to have a chance at escape. However, since we're confined to this compartment most of the day, the only way we'll know is when we're on deck. That's a very narrow window of time."

"You're right about the exceptionally iffy. Explain how you're certain we can overpower the guards since neither you nor I are special forces material."

Wayan did.

The RQ-4 Global Hawk is a high-altitude, remotely piloted surveillance aircraft over fifteen feet in height, forty-eight feet in width, and has a wingspan of one hundred thirty-one feet. Able to stay aloft for up to forty-two hours and survey forty thousand square miles of terrain a day, the complex aircraft has a crew of three—the launch and recovery element (LRE), the mission control element (MCE), and the sensor operator. Once the LRE pilot got the Global Hawk airborne, the MCE assumed control during the mission phase of the operation, returning it to the LRE when it was time to land.

Three RQ-4 UAVs were stationed at a secret drone base in a desolate area of southeast Saudi Arabia known as Rub al-Khali, each housed in a clamshell-shaped hangar. Two were unassigned, and one was on a mission. Upon leaving McInnes's office and returning to her desk, Parra tasked the two available RQ-4 UAVs. One would inspect Scops Island, while the other examined the oil platform at the coordinates Ock gave Cheup.

While the crew was performing pre-flight checks before towing the UAVs from their hangars, Parra spoke to the MCEs. The pilot taking the drone to Facility Number One had two mission directives. The first was to visually and electronically surveil the tiny island, and the second was to hover above it and report any vessel approaching or leaving its dock. In the latter situation, the pilot would provide the ship's course and speed once it was underway. The MCE of the drone going to the oil platform had one mission directive: keep it under constant electronic and visual surveillance.

It was one thousand four hundred twenty-three miles between Scops Island and Rub al-Khali, and one thousand three hundred forty miles between the airbase and the oil platform. The first Global Hawk would take approximately four hours to reach the island, and the second a little under that to arrive at the platform—both times ten percent of their remain-aloft capability. The LRE, MCE, and sensor operator controlled the aircraft via satellite link from Creech Air Force Base in Nevada. Although the distance to the oil platform was marginally shorter, the Scops drone was the first to arrive, prepped for flight before its brother.

When the RQ-4 arrived at Facility Number One, it entered a circular holding pattern at forty thousand feet, well below its sixty-five thousand feet ceiling. After establishing a link with the Aerospace Data Facility at Buckley Air Force Base in Colorado, it began transmitting video and electronic surveillance data. Libby Parra received the same data over a special-access link, displaying it on separate LED screens in the center of her desk.

Her first look at the island showed dense jungle surrounding a cleared rectangular area. Within this area was what appeared to be a large residence. Fifty yards to its right were a dozen small structures that resembled bungalows. To the left of the residence were a pair of three-story buildings. On the backside of this grouping were a sewage treatment plant, a solar farm, and another building with large pipes extending into the ocean, which she guessed was a desalination plant. Near it was a cluster of white satellite domes. A fifty-foot-wide dock, which looked sturdy enough to drive tanks or other heavy equipment across, extended some distance into the ocean. Beside it was a heavy-lift crane.

The drone's electronic surveillance detected two walkie-talkie conversations, which went through a Korean-to-English translation program before appearing on Parra's screen. Both were discussions regarding logistical matters within the facility. Parra had no idea what they were talking about but would find an expert who would.

Ten minutes after she received the first images of Scops Island, the second Global Hawk arrived at the platform. The images on her monitor were so sharp she could read the signs posted on the platform. As she looked at the workers on the main deck, she was unprepared for what she saw. Something was seriously wrong. She called McInnes.

October 13, 2021—onboard the Bolt Hole

Melis Woo wasn't the patient or forgiving type. It wasn't in her nature, and she wasn't going to change her ways. The email she received from Kim Jong-un informed her the dictator would not comply with her demands and would kill the private investigators if she told anyone about Scops Island. He'd called her bluff and won, correctly guessing she wouldn't follow through with her threat because that would mean certain death for the very people she was trying to protect.

She knew Kim Jong-un couldn't be trusted because she'd worked for him and didn't find a shred of humanity in the narcissist prick. There was no way he was going to release Wayan and Endah. They were his only link to her, and he was going to interrogate them to within an inch of death to discover where she'd hidden his money. When he learned they didn't know, he'd finish the job. Regardless, he'd close the facility because he could never be sure she wouldn't reveal its location. Therefore, she needed a permanent resolution to save the private investigators and keep him from coming after them again. That excluded returning his money. Even after getting it back, he'd come after the three of them because his mindset was to retaliate against anyone who tried to harm or take advantage of him. Therefore, giving the money back wasn't a solution.

Woo picked up her Toughbook laptop lying on the deck beside her chair and logged into her browser. Her thoughts were elsewhere, and she typed the wrong symbol as part of her password, generating a denial of entry warning. As she corrected her mistake, it came to her how she could save Wayan and Endah's lives and keep Kim Jong-un from coming after them in the future.

When washing money for the dictator, she had unlimited access to North Korea's offshore bank accounts because she'd set them up and funneled cash in and out of them depending on the country's needs. That's how she cleaned out his treasury so quickly, even though there were stringent security procedures in place. Each time she accessed these accounts, she required an RSA decryption key. Three devices only produced these. Her former boss, Kulon Sanadi, had one. If he weren't around, she'd get it from General Kang in Beijing. As a last resort, she'd ask an assistant to Kim Jong-un, who had the third device. Upon receiving the key, she had sixty seconds to enter the alpha-numeric code, or she needed to request another. She knew Sanadi kept his device taped to the underside of his desk. She'd seen him remove it on more than one occasion, and she took it the day she fled Hong Kong. She speculated he didn't keep the device in a safe or locked in a drawer because he was constantly in and out of the computer system, and there were guards in the office. Everyone needed an RSA decryption key to access the system. Without it, as Sanadi told her, only the NSA could hack it.

Prior to a few seconds ago, the last time she thought about

the RSA device was when she used it to empty Kim Jong-un's coffers. Stored in her safe, she didn't know whether it worked or had been deactivated. However, with Sanadi and Kang dead, the deactivation process needed to come from one of Kim Jong-un's assistants because the dictator was a big picture person and not into administrative details. Terrified they'd screw up; the assistants may not have thought about it or were too scared to pull the plug on something they weren't asked about. If it was still active, she had a way to guarantee not only her safety but that of Wayan and Endah now and in the future.

CHAPTER 11

McInnes shook his head as he looked at the images of the oil platform taken by the RQ-4. "This can't be it," he said, turning his gaze to Parra, who was standing to the left of his desk chair. "It's an active drilling rig. You said an oil and gas company in India owns it?"

"It's a public company that has no known ties with North Korea, Iran, or terrorist groups. This isn't the platform we're looking for."

"Did Ock give the ship's captain the wrong coordinates?" McInnes asked.

"What are the odds the wrong coordinates would be another oil platform and not a spot of open water in the Arabian Sea? This was deliberate subterfuge. Do you recall the conversation between Ock and the ship's captain, where he asked Cheup to authenticate bravo?"

"I recall."

"I think it was a challenge-response authentication. What if bravo was a pre-arranged signal to switch the vessel's destination? This could be as easy as the captain going to his safe and opening a sealed envelope that contained the platform's location. Bravo could also signal Cheup to ignore the verbal coordinates and proceed to a spot he already knew. It doesn't matter how they changed the ship's destination; the Global Hawk is in the wrong place."

"Just another day in intelligence—sorting out what's real and what's not."

"When I began working here, the former director told me what we do is not unlike gathering a novel that had been disassembled into separate sentences and thrown onto the floor. Our job is to gather and re-assemble it—not knowing the plot or the characters."

"That's a good analogy. Have we accumulated the sentences to re-assemble that novel?"

"We're getting there. We know the object of our search is a platform in the Arabian Sea."

"Any idea how we find the platform? The Arabian Sea adjoins the Indian Ocean. They'll be a multitude of offshore platforms."

"We can narrow that number down significantly by searching for those which have been decommissioned because launching an ICBM off an active oil rig would risk triggering an explosion that would destroy the missile. However, it may be too early to find the platform."

"Explain to someone without your analytical prowess why we're too early."

"The preliminary data shows there are over eight hundred platforms in the Arabian Sea. If you exclude active ones, it's still a big number—too big to send drones to look at each. Even if we find the right one, we may not know it unless there's activity on the decommissioned platform. The best way to confirm we have the right one is when the ships carrying the Hwasong-16's and launchers dock there."

"That makes sense," McInnes acknowledged. "Since overcoming insurmountable problems with little to go on and time running short is normal for you, how do we find the platform?"

"By making the invisible, visible," Parra said before explaining what she meant.

As McInnes and Parra were speaking, another ship was navigating towards the oil platform near the Yemeni island of Socotra. The Iranian vessel flew a Panamanian flag at sea and had a Saudi name on its bow. Dispatched from the Persian port of Chabahar, which was on the coast of the Gulf of Oman and the southernmost city in Iran, it transported the missile's fuel and oxidizer.

The vessel was a chameleon of sorts, constructed to appear as a nondescript merchant ship, having cranes and hoists on its deck to enhance that impression. Below deck, it was a model of sophistication maintaining the highly volatile liquid hydrogen missile fuel at minus four hundred twenty-three degrees Fahrenheit. Keeping the temperature constant was critical because if it rose or the pressure within its storage container decreased from the thirteen times normal atmospheric pressure at which it was maintained, the fuel would evaporate and return to a gaseous state. Since hydrogen is highly explosive, no one aboard the ship wanted to see if the ventilation and pressure relief values functioned as designed. The ship also transported liquid oxygen, an oxidizer that required storage at minus two hundred ninety-eight degrees Fahrenheit for the oxygen to remain in its liquid state. It enabled the rocket fuel to burn.

The Iranian vessel, the Hao Chang, and the Ja Ryu, now the Morning Sun, were scheduled to arrive at the platform on October 18th.

The technicians and support equipment sent by Major General Hassani arrived at the platform two weeks prior to the ship's arrivals. There was an enormous amount of work to do— installing the wiring, communication systems, junction boxes, generators, ducting, and other infrastructure necessities. He could have started the process earlier. However, he didn't want to risk accidentally exposing the platform's location. That would be catastrophic. Therefore, he put together an aggressive 24/7 work schedule.

According to his latest communication with Ock, the launch pads would arrive slightly ahead of the other vessels, where they would be lifted from the ship's hold by the platform crane and secured to the main deck. Shortly after that, the Hao Chang would arrive, and its missiles placed on the launchers. The ship carrying the fuel would dock at approximately the same time, and the fuel and oxidizer ducts connected to its storage tanks. Fueling the five missiles was unavoidably time-consuming because of the large amount of liquid hydrogen and oxidizer required, taking approximately three hours to fill each ICBM.

To minimize detection, Ock and Hassani disabled their ship's automatic identification system or AIS, which worked in an autonomous mode and displayed the vessel's data on an electronic chart display and information system, or ECDIS. Replacing paper charts, it provided navigational data, traffic, and hazards in the surrounding area. However, the AIS wasn't disabled for this reason. They took it offline because its transceiver attached a unique identifier to a vessel, along with its position, course, and speed. Once switched off, the ship became invisible at sea—or so each of the captains of the three ships headed for the platform believed.

Following his call with McInnes, Abe Talman's heart raced, being told by the head of the NSA of the possible launch of twenty nuclear warheads at Israel. Although McInnes was clear the missiles could also be carrying a sizeable conventional warhead, he didn't believe for a moment that Iran would go to all this trouble to hide the launch site unless they were planning a nuclear attack. He was irritated at the four-star general for not revealing the exact location of the oil platform, although he said it was in the Arabian Sea. McInnes feared he'd make a preemptive strike against the platform before the missiles and warheads arrived. That belief was correct. Israel wouldn't exist if he waited to have every bit of information in front of him before setting the military loose on a target. The country's survival depended on preemptive rather than retaliatory strikes. Sometimes they got it wrong and struck a non-strategic target. However, most of the time, they hit the bullseye.

With Israel's existence in question, he needed to find and destroy the platform before the Iranians could launch an attack. Once destroyed, he'd search for the vessels carrying the missiles and the launchers. They had to be in the vicinity. He called his chief of planning, tasking him to assemble a list of platforms in the Arabian Sea and eliminate active ones. Once compiled, he was to lay them out in grid patterns so that drones could efficiently look at each.

Talman's primary limitation in searching for the platform was that only the Eitan drone, which had a range of nearly two thousand eight hundred miles and could stay aloft for up to thirty-six hours, had the range to cover the area in question. However, if launched from airbases in Israel, they wouldn't have sufficient fuel to return to Israel. Usually, he'd ask the United States for permission to refuel the drones at one of its middle eastern airstrips. They'd always granted his previous requests. This time, he suspected otherwise. Once McInnes learned of the refueling request, he'd figure out what the Mossad was up to and deny him the fuel until the ships docked at the platform. By then, he believed, Israel's existence would be hanging by a thread—the push of a launch button away from annihilation.

Israel needed a friendly country near the Arabian Sea—the closer, the better, to refuel its drones. Since Talman couldn't ask the United States, he had only one choice—Ethiopia, the most populous landlocked country in the world. The two nations had excellent diplomatic relations, with Israel providing ongoing military assistance. He made the call.

The data displayed on the two desktop screens on the NSA director's desk resulted from a program written by one of Parra's uber-geeks, taking and integrating the data from an NSA imaging satellite and the ECDIS system, which were both surveilling the Arabian Sea. Red and green dots populated one of those screens, the green representing ships with an AIS transceiver signal, and the red those without. Images of the vessels, which could be expanded with the click of a mouse, were on the other.

"I count twenty-six vessels without identities," McInnes said.

"Fourteen ships," Parra said, pointing to the LED monitor and expanding those images, "are fishing vessels which are probably in the waters of another country. They're not large enough to carry either the missiles or launchers. Another five are small merchant vessels. It's unknown why their transceivers are down. They could be broken."

"That leaves seven."

"These seven ships are between three hundred fifty and one thousand three hundred feet in length. None are flying the North Korean flag."

"I know that look, Libby," McInnes said, seeing the mischievous grin on her face, experience telling him she had found what she was after but wanted him to know that getting there hadn't been easy.

"Taking the names on the vessels and researching their ownership and the flags they're flying, one was a Russian Federation spying vessel, which we've long known about, and two were flying the Venezuelan flag and were getting around their country's embargo by importing oil from Iran. Both ships don't have the large deck openings necessary to load and offload something as huge as an ICBM or its launcher."

"That leaves four."

"The Hao Chang is flying the South Korean Flag. It's registered to a South Korean company that chartered it to an offshore corporation purporting to transport goods around the middle east. According to the owner, the AIS transceiver was working at the time of the charter. The Korean company must have been satisfied with the lessee's financial wherewithal before turning over their ship. This vessel can easily transport the missiles."

"Smugglers?"

"It's a big ship for smugglers. Its AIS malfunction could be a legitimate maintenance issue. The next ship is the Abby Aurora, which is flying a Panamanian flag. It doesn't exist in any ship's registry. It's going southeast towards the tip of India. The third vessel is the Morning Sun. Its name also doesn't appear in any ship's registry."

"And the last one?"

"The Bahri Ghazal is flying the flag of Saudi Arabia, and Bahri is a common first name for a Saudi-owned nautical carrier. However, another ship bearing this name is transmitting an AIS signal from the Dead Sea."

"Follow all of them," McInnes said.

"I already am."

CHAPTER 12

"We're agreed. If we don't get off this ship, we're as good as dead not long after we pull into a North Korean port and Kim Jong-un gets his hands on us," Wayan said in a low voice so that those outside their compartment couldn't hear what they were saying.

"I'd rather be killed trying to escape."

"That's our advantage."

"Being killed while escaping?"

"As we said, if Kim Jong-un wanted us dead, we wouldn't be on this ship. I'm guessing anyone who kills us would face a similar fate from him—and the captain and crew know it," Wayan stated.

"You're right. We're eating well and not being abused."

"To be clear, even if we overpower the four guards and lower a lifeboat in the water, we don't know how close we are to land or a shipping lane. We're adrift hoping for a miracle."

"It's better than the certainty of being tortured and killed by that butcher," Eka said. "I'd do it if for no other reason than denying him the satisfaction of murdering us."

"Knowing his temper, not giving him that pleasure will make him blow a fuse."

The comment brought a smile from Eka.

"I figure nighttime works best because most of the crew will be asleep."

"Any idea how we get the lifeboat into the water without the crew stopping us?"

"None."

"I know you'll come up with a plan."

"That sounds singular."

"You're the brains of the outfit."

"We can argue the truth of that statement later—assuming we're alive to discuss it. For now, we both better get creative."

The Abby Aurora had the pedal to the metal, which meant it was going around seventeen mph. Forty thousand feet over it, the Global Hawk that previously provided imagery for Scops Island was following it. Its sister RQ-4 was re-tasked from photographing the working oil platform to monitoring the Morning Sun, formerly the Ja Ryu. Both aircraft were long-endurance drones.

Parra liked the Global Hawk because it had the Processing, Exploitation, and Dissemination system—PED. The advanced algorithms incorporated into it sifted through the video feed and sensors to identify moments of human relevance, cross-referencing intelligence data in the process. Therefore, an analyst didn't need to look at every second of the drone's video for fear of missing something. The PED would bring it to their attention.

Because Northrop Grumman only manufactured forty-two RQ-4's, the two hundred twenty million dollar drones were always in heavy demand. Parra tried but couldn't get ahold of another because the others were already tasked. However, she laid her hands on two MQ-9 Reaper drones out of Thumrait Air Base in Tamarid, Oman, whose pilots were at Creech. One aircraft was ordered to follow the Bahri Ghazal, and the other the Hao Chang. She gave Creech operations the general area where they might find these vessels. Since Oman bordered the Arabian Sea, the Reaper's one thousand one hundred fifty mile range and fourteen hours of airborne time made it a good, if not the only choice, for surveilling the area where these ships were believed to be traveling.

The US Air Force had five bases in Oman. If surveillance continued beyond fourteen hours, which was one-third the time an RQ-4 could remain aloft, replacement Reapers could quickly be launched from one of these bases. At thirty-two million dollars an aircraft, fifteen percent the cost of a Global Hawk, the military had one hundred ninety-five Reapers. A considerable number of these workhorse drones were based in the Middle East.

October 14, 2021—over the Indian Ocean

While the Global Hawk's surveilled the Abby Aurora, the data stream from its imaging, electro-optical radar, signal intelligence sensors, and scanned array radar was transmitted to a satellite in the US Department of Defense Wideband Global Satcom (WGS) constellation at three hundred megabits per second. From there, the data was routed at a similarly high speed through the DOD network, appearing virtually real-time on the pilot's console at of the 432nd Air Expeditionary Wing at Creech Air Force Base in Nevada. When the pilot saw the sensor data, he summoned the operations officer.

"There's no hiding from a Global Hawk," the ops officer said. He kicked what he saw up the chain of command and called the wing commander.

"You might be interested to know," the colonel said in a tone tinged with anxiety as he spoke to McInnes, who had Parra standing beside him, "that the hawk's sensors penetrated the deck of the Abby Aurora and discovered it was transporting five ICBM-sized missiles and, unless it's headed for a conehead convention, a corresponding number of MIRVs."

"Is the Global Hawk armed?" Parra asked.

"No," the colonel answered.

"Can you get an armed drone airborne, and have it put a huge hole in the Abby Aurora below the waterline?" McInnes asked.

"Have someone cut the orders, and I'll send a Reaper from Oman. It will take around three hours to punch that hole in the vessel."

"You'll get your authority from the NCA in a few minutes."

The three Eitan drones left the Tel Nof Air Base, also known as Air Force Base 8, near Rehovat, Israel, and landed in Ethiopia after receiving approval to operate from one of the country's airfields. That was a good thing since Talman ordered them and a support aircraft airborne before getting the Ethiopian government's permission, and the drones didn't have enough fuel to return to Israel if their refueling request was denied. The Israeli Air Force C-130J Super Hercules, carrying support staff and spare parts, had a top speed that was one hundred fifty mph more than an Eitan and touched down ahead of the drones.

Once the drones landed and taxied to the parking ramp, the support crew refueled them and, minutes later, the aircraft returned to the runway and lifted off. The pilots were at the Tel Nof Air Base, and each was given a grid to search, looking for non-active oil platforms that could accommodate five Hwasong-16 missiles and their launchers. Although an Eitan could stay aloft for up to thirty-six hours, Israeli air force regulations dictated that drone pilots could only be at their controls for a maximum of twelve. Subsequently, they often worked in tandem, relieving each other every eight to twelve hours, the length of a shift depending on the availability of pilots.

Twelve hours and thirty minutes into one of the drone's grid patterns, the Eitan operating off the coast of Yemen sent back images of a huge oil platform that appeared derelict. It was the sixth such platform that the Eitan's discovered. What made this one unique were the thick cables stretching across the deck and the insulated ducting extending from the main deck to sea level. Moreover, the pilot saw faint wisps of white smoke vented from the side of the platform. He'd seen similar emissions on previous missions, analysts later explaining these either came from diesel that had not been appropriately combusted in the engine cylinders or steam from the water in the fuel. Either way, the pilot knew this platform wasn't as derelict as someone would have them believe. If it weren't for the drone's powerful thermographic camera, he would never have seen the nearly invisible wisps of smoke. The pilot notified his squadron commander, who ran to the operations center and looked over his shoulder at the LED screen. There was no mistaking the images he was seeing. The commander immediately called the head of Mossad.

Abe Talman studied the drone images of the platform sent to him. Having questions on what he was seeing, he called the director of the Shavit rocket program at the Israeli Space Agency, or ISA, which was part of the Ministry of Science and Technology.

The ISA director, who had known Talman for nearly two decades, listened to what he had to say before responding. " You want me to drop what I'm doing and come to your office? I have a launch coming up, and I'm chasing my tail."

"I have a video that I need you to look at."

"Send it to me. I can receive secure emails. I'll look at it on my computer while we talk."

"It's too sensitive. The data must stay in my office for now. I wouldn't ask if it wasn't crucial."

"I'll get my driver," the ISA director said, in a tone that indicated a reluctant acquiescence.

"Tell him to hurry; time isn't our friend."

"It never is." Twenty-five minutes later, he stepped into Talman's office.

"Tell me what you see in this video?" Talman asked, not bothering with small talk as he hit the play button on his remote.

"This is extremely clear," the ISA director said as he looked at the video monitor. "Our video or the American's?"

"Ours," Talman answered.

"Impressive."

The video continued for five minutes, after which Talman stopped it, hit the rewind key, and zoomed in on a large duct.

"What can you tell me about this?"

"It's designed to carry extremely cold fluid."

"How do you know?"

"The duct is encased in cryogenic insulation," the scientist said. "The ISA also uses it."

"What's cryogenic insulation?"

"It's laminated densified wood impregnated with synthetic resin in a vacuum. You'll see what I'm talking about here," the scientist said, hitting play on the remote before stopping it thirty seconds later. "This shows a cross-section of the insulation that's been trimmed away."

"You used the words extremely cold. How cold is that?"

"The liquid in our insulated conduits can be as low as minus four hundred twenty-three degrees Fahrenheit."

"Why would you need anything at a temperature that low?" Talman asked, clearly puzzled.

"To keep something that's naturally a gas in a liquid state—such as hydrogen."

"Give me a use."

"We pump missile fuel through our conduit."

Talman's face lit up. He'd found what he was looking for.

The escape plan was far from perfect, but they decided imperfect would have to do since it was all they had. Setting the sequence of what needed to happen, they started with the door—which could only be unlocked outside. The guards only did this when they brought meals, escorted them on deck, or took them to the bathroom. At night, because Wayan's prostrate was ten years past its prime, they accompanied him there every three or four hours.

Once outside their compartment, and assuming they overpowered the two guards stationed beside the door, they had to get past the sentry at the end of the passageway. The same problem confronted them with the fourth guard, who stood in front of the ladder leading to the deck above.

If they incapacitated the four guards and reached the main deck before anyone sounded the alarm, which Wayan quipped even Las Vegas wouldn't take as a bet; neither he nor Eka knew how to lower one of the ship's lifeboats, although they'd seen the controls when walking past them.

"Any ideas?" Wayan asked.

"Have you ever been on a cruise ship?"

"No."

"They have lifeboat drills, and I've seen them being lowered, although those were closed lifeboats. The ones on this ship are open—not much different than those you saw in the movie *Moby Dick*.

"I never saw it."

"Surprising, you can buy it in a comic book format with large print."

"The point?" Wayan impatiently asked.

"I'm not sure how to release these lifeboats, but I can tell you about the procedure on the cruise ship."

"That might be close enough. Take me through it."

"They take off the lines, hooks, and straps—everything connecting it to the boat. They then pull a handle, which gently lowers it to the water."

"Sounds simple."

"They might have done a few things I didn't see. It's probably a more complicated process."

"With our luck, it will be significantly more complicated. We'll likely be moving. There's no guarantee the lifeboat wouldn't flip or disintegrate upon impact with the water."

"We need a lot of luck to pull this off, Wayan."

"I know. So far, that's been in short supply."

Parra and McInnes were speaking with the MQ-9 pilot who sent the Abby Aurora to the bottom of the Indian Ocean. He explained his Reaper carried fourteen AGM-114 Hellfire missiles and two GBU-12 Paveway laser-guided bombs on the six pylons under its wings.

"I didn't believe the Hellfire missile, an anti-armor weapon designed to destroy anything from a car to a tank, would inflict enough damage to sink the ship. Therefore, I used the Paveway, a smart bomb with a five hundred pound warhead. It struck the forward part of the main deck," the pilot said.

"And the ship sank," McInnes volunteered.

"No. The explosion created a large hole, and the vessel lost power. The ship was on fire, but it wasn't listing. Therefore, I released the second Paveway. When it hit, the center of the ship split apart, with the halves sinking rapidly. I saw no survivors."

"Was there a secondary explosion?" McInnes asked.

"None that I saw, sir."

Parra and McInnes felt they had what they needed and ended the call after thanking the pilot.

"Give the Navy the coordinates of where it sank," McInnes said. "They'll want to recover the MIRVs and missiles, or pieces of them."

Parra said she'd take care of it.

"What else do you have?" the NSA director asked, looking at the folder in her hands.

"These are the below-deck images sent by the RQ-4 following the Morning Sun," Parra said, withdrawing several photos and handing them to him. "It's carrying five transporter-erector-launchers."

"Not much use without the missiles."

"What if the Abby Aurora wasn't the only ship carrying missiles and MIRVs?"

"What are you thinking?"

"The three other vessels we're tracking are going in the opposite direction from the Abby Aurora. Interestingly, they seem to be on a course to converge west of Yemen. What if the Bahri Ghazal or the

Hao Chang are also carrying missiles and warheads? The only way to be sure they aren't, is to get images of what's below their decks."

McInnes's face showed his concern. "How long will it take to get a Global Hawk over those ships?"

"In the neighborhood of three hours."

"Make it happen."

Kim Jong-un didn't take bad news well, and it was not unknown for him to kill the messenger of such tidings. A junior lieutenant, the lowest officer rank in the army, was tasked to deliver the message of the Abby Aurora's demise. The young officer, who was skinny to the point of appearing malnourished, and wore black glasses with thick frames, was seventeen years of age. He trembled as he handed the envelope containing the message to the supreme leader. Although he didn't know what was in it, he figured it wasn't good from the expression on his superior's face and that no one of rank wanted to give it to the dictator.

The junior lieutenant was shaking as he handed over the envelope, rapidly leaving the room after he did. As soon as he was out of sight, he ran to the car which brought him to the palace—wanting to get as far away as possible before the envelope was opened.

The dictator ripped apart the gold privacy seal across the envelope's flap and removed and unfolded the single sheet of paper within. *The Abby Aurora has been attacked. We've lost power and,* was all the message said before abruptly ending. A note below indicated the precise time it was received. Kim Jong-un crumpled the paper into a wad the size of a ping pong ball and threw it across his office. His face turned red, and he followed that toss by taking a delicate porcelain ashtray off his desk and hurling it in the same direction, two of his staff ducking as it sailed past. Hitting the wall behind them, it disintegrated into a multitude of shards.

"That bitch told the Americans," he screamed.

CHAPTER 13

October 15, 2021—Washington, DC

The director of national intelligence, Thomas Winegar, was a Kansas native. In Washington, where *go along to get along* was a mantra, he was a breath of fresh air for anyone who wanted the politics removed from the advice they were given. He spoke with a slight midwestern drawl and was looked upon as the Mark Twain of the National Security Council. There were several reasons for this. He had the slightly disheveled look of an Einstein or Twain, his hair was completely white, even though he was in his 50s, and he had a commonsense approach to complex issues and good-natured humor when trying to get his point across. Sitting beside him in a conference room in the Pentagon's National Military Command Center, referred to as the NMCC, the command and communications hub for the National Command Authority, was Secretary of Defense Jim Rosen. The ex-Marine general, who kept his hair high and tight at age sixty-two and had a booming voice, turned down several lucrative jobs within the defense industry to become SecDef.

Since the NSA was part of the Department of Defense, McInnes sent Rosen the RQ-4 and MQ-9 data and imagery, along with a capsulized analysis. Upon receiving the information, SecDef called the DNI and asked Winegar to come to his office at the Pentagon. Although Rosen could have asked the opinion of the joint chiefs and left the DNI out of the loop, that was short-sighted. The DOD and the alphabet agencies under the DNI's control, such as the CIA and DIA, worked in concert to protect the nation's interests, and he had to get him up to speed in the event they needed to act quickly. He might get additional perspectives from the joint chiefs, which was always good in decision-making. However, he didn't want to risk paralysis by analysis. The military was large and complex. Experience taught him that consulting with the four-star in each branch, who wanted to prove their command's value, sometimes complicated the situation. Therefore, he decided to exclude them for the moment and have a one-on-one conversation with Winegar and see where that led.

When Winegar arrived, Rosen showed him what he received from the NSA. It didn't take them long to come to a consensus.

"McInnes isn't going to be happy," Rosen said.

"Our jobs seldom give anyone a ray of sunshine. We're here to keep those we've sworn to protect from getting hit by a bolt of lightning during a thunderstorm, even though they might be drenched and holding a steel rod."

"Which means the lightning sometimes strikes us," Rosen replied.

"How will he take it?"

"He's military. He'll suck it up and soldier on."

"It still sucks."

Rosen initiated a video conference, and McInnes and Parra appeared on the large LED screen mounted on the wall of the SecDef's office. After a brief exchange of pleasantries, Rosen asked the NSA director to recap the analysis sent to him.

"Iran's supreme leader, and a cadre of chief advisors, have been discretely moving to the Fordhow fuel enrichment plant, which is ninety miles from Tehran," he began. "That's a former Islamic Revolutionary Guard Corps center that's deep within a mountain near the village of Fordhow."

"They've gone there in the past when they believe Tehran could be the target of a retaliatory attack," Winegar said.

"Meaning a nation sends a cruise missile or special forces team to take them out of the equation following an attack on their interests or people," Rosen added.

"That's correct. In this instance, we believe they're at Fordhow because they intend to launch five ICBMs at Israel, each capable of carrying a MIRV." McInnes explained this assumption was based on the NSAs analysis of North Korean intercepts and the sinking of the Abby Aurora, which was detected carrying ICBMs and warheads.

Winegar nodded, having read the summary.

"You sank the ship carrying the missiles and warheads," Rosen stated. "Do the Iranians and North Koreans know these strategic weapons are at the bottom of the ocean?"

"We're not sure about the Iranians, but the North Koreas are aware of the destruction of the Abby Aurora. We intercepted a Satcom transmission from the vessel to a military communications center in Pyongyang just before the second Paveway bomb struck. It stated the ship was attacked and lost power, after which the transmission abruptly ended. However, we don't believe these missiles were going to be launched at Israel or American forces in the Middle East."

"Why?" Rosen asked, that conclusion not in the NSA summary.

"The Abby Aurora was going south. That's in the opposite direction of the Arabian Sea, which our intercepts give as the location of the platform where the Hwasong-16's were headed."

"There's another vessel transporting similar weapons?" Winegar asked.

"That's our belief."

"How many ships are you looking for?" Winegar asked.

"We've narrowed it to three. When we find them, we'll get an image of what's below their decks. Extrapolating their last known directions, they'll converge at what we believe will be the area in which the Arabian Sea platform is located."

"You don't have the precise convergent coordinates, or you wouldn't need to follow the ships," Winegar said.

"They're so far from where they'll converge that all we have is a general area and not a set of coordinates for the platform. The closer they get to one another, the narrower the area and the more accurate our prediction of the platform's location."

"What's the size of the area?"

"A hundred miles to a side."

"That's ten thousand square miles."

"If we find the ships or platform and detect strategic weapons on one or more of them, we'll request authorization to destroy the missiles."

"Do you believe Israel is the target?" Rosen asked.

"The destruction of Israel is a national priority for Iran."

"They also have a hatred for America. In the past, they've launched missiles at US troops in Iraq."

"But not the destructive power of five ICBMs. Hitting US troops or our territory with this large an attack would galvanize the American public and generate overwhelming support for a powerful response." McInnes said.

"If Iran fired five conventional warheads at American interests or its citizens, they'd be pumping oil by hand for a generation, and we'd reduce their military capabilities to below that of the Vatican," Rosen stated. "If they up the stakes and launch nuclear missiles at us—they'll cease to be a functioning country. We may get a bloody nose, but they'll be taken to the morgue."

"Never underestimate religious zealots. They drink their own Kool-Aid," Winegar added.

McInnes conceded that underestimating any adversary is a mistake.

Rosen stepped in. "That's solid work," he said. "However, I have a problem, and the only way to solve it is by using your four drones."

McInnes's face hardened. Parra, seated beside him, mirrored that expression.

"You're taking the drones?" the NSA director said.

"I don't have a choice, Parker. I need them to blanket Iran's coastal and fringe areas not covered by our Keyhole satellites. Your drones are in the area and airborne."

"I told you it's the NSA's assessment that one or more ships are carrying missiles and warheads towards the Arabian Sea with Israel as the probable target. There's no way to find them without UAVs. Take three drones; leave me one."

"I'm not sure your four will be enough. I may have to pull others from operational assignments. Thanks to the hard work of the NSA, the DNI and I agree with your conclusion that Iran is about to launch a conventional or nuclear missile attack. However, we don't share your certainty that it's Israel. The target may be one of our Middle Eastern assets, mirroring the previous attack against the Al Asad base in Iraq on a much larger scale. I want to make it clear that I'm not abandoning you. I'm reassigning MQ-9 replacement drones that are currently over the Sudan and Chad. When they return to their base in Oman and are serviced and refueled, you can continue your search."

"How long will that be?" McInnes asked.

"Twenty-four hours."

McInnes didn't like giving up his drones, but he didn't have a choice given the NSA was part of the Department of Defense, and Rosen was his boss. Under normal circumstances, when the DOD was short on UAV resources, they'd go to the CIA and call in one of the chits they owed for off-the-books favors or offer a chit for future services. However, that wasn't going to work because Winegar was the director of national intelligence and the CIA fell under his purview. With Rosen and Winegar working in concert, there was no way they were getting a drone from any of the agencies or departments under their umbrellas.

"What's the chance of finding those ships a day from now?" McInnes asked Parra.

"About the same as a congressperson inviting you to dinner and picking up the tab."

"That's what I thought."

"There might be a way to get a UAV sooner," Parra said, getting McInnes's attention. "Jim Goodburn owes me a big favor for exposing two Soviet-era nuclear weapons before terrorists could use them to level Beijing and Shanghai. It made him a hero to the Chinese president. As the National Security Advisor, when he asks for a resource, everyone assumes it's at the president's request. He might be able to get us a drone or two."

"It's worth a try."

Parra called Goodburn. Stuck in meetings, it took two hours to get ahold of him. With a doctorate in terrorism and cybersecurity from Georgetown, the NSC director was a senior fellow at a Washington think tank for twenty-two years before the president asked him to serve in his administration. The Iowa native was straight-spoken, not prone to ambiguities, and had an excellent memory—unlike most in the nation's capital who developed amnesia on promised reciprocity soon after being given a favor. Parra explained the situation.

"Winegar and Rosen are briefing the NSC in an hour. Honestly, I don't disagree with them or you, and both sides have solid arguments for use of the drones."

"Does that mean you're staying out of this, and the NSA is on the sideline watching for twenty-four hours?" Parra asked.

"This isn't about the UAVs; this is about using available resources to protect our country, its citizens, and treaty allies. If Winegar or Rosen came to me with a request for drones, I would give them the same response I'm giving you."

"Which is?"

"Give me a minute." Goodburn was silent, and McInnes and Parra could hear him typing on his keyboard. Two minutes later, he resumed their conversation. "I can give you two armed MQ-9 Reaper drones based at Baledogle Airfield in Somalia. I wish I could provide another two, but that's all I can get on short notice."

"Baledogle is a CIA operation."

"It's a former Soviet airport that serves the Somali Air Force, and the CIA operates Reaper drones from there to employ against Al-Shabaab militants."

"When the CIA field agent tells Winegar that the NSA is using their drones, and he tells Rosen, you'll be the first person to get my resume when I'm job hunting."

"When the NSC asks for a drone, the CIA assumes it's being used in a black op authorized by the president. They don't ask questions because these operations are classified, and only those with a need to know are read in. That's protocol. The CIA's pilots are in a separate area of the Creech operations center, with no one permitted near them during the mission. Each is in a separate cube. You'll be the only one they'll speak with."

"How soon can we have the drones?"

"Now."

CHAPTER 14

October 16, 2021—Mossad headquarters, Tel Aviv, Israel

Once Talman decided the platform discovered by the Eitan drone posed an existential threat to the safety of Israel and should be destroyed, he needed to get authorization from the prime minister who, if he approved, would direct the minister of defense to send assets to destroy it.

During his call with the prime minister, he detailed his conversation with the NSA and sent the photographs taken by the Eitan. The head of the Israeli government, accustomed to acting quickly on intel because the nation's survival often depended on it, subsequently had a video conference with the National Security Council—which was organizationally a part of his office. The meeting took twenty minutes, after which there was unanimous agreement with Talman's recommendation to destroy the platform.

Protocol next dictated that the prime minister briefs his cabinet and gain their support for the strategic attack. He didn't require unanimous approval because only he and the defense minister had to agree to the attack. However, if a majority voiced their support, there would be minimal political ramifications if something went wrong. For most governments, this process would be lengthy. In Israel, it took less than two hours. The prime minister then phoned the defense minister, and with his concurrence, the action was approved.

The minister had three ways to conduct an attack beyond Israel's borders. Since the platform in question was two thousand four hundred seventeen miles from Tel Aviv, the first was to arm an Eitan drone with air-to-surface missiles. Although the country never acknowledged its UAVs carried weapons, it was an open secret they did. The Eitan could destroy the platform, but using it required launching the attack from Ethiopia because of the UAV's limited range. While that government had no issue letting Israeli reconnaissance drones use its airbases, it made clear that launching an attack from them would end their relationship. Unwilling to lose a key ally in the region, the prime minister eliminated this consideration.

The second possibility was to use a warship. These were on patrol in the Mediterranean Sea, the Gulf of Aqaba, and the Red Sea. None of these patrol areas was remotely near the platform, and getting assets close enough to initiate an attack would take time. Additionally, since the satellites of several nations constantly monitor naval movements, redirecting maritime assets might provide an early warning to those on the oil platform from a nation friendly with Iran. Subsequently, this consideration was eliminated by the minister of defense. That left only one option: have the air force blow the platform out of existence.

Two F-35I Lightning II aircraft, a fifth-generation single-engine strike fighter developed by the United States that incorporated cutting-edge stealth technology, were selected to conduct the attack. Each plane would carry two Rampage missiles. The fifteen feet long, one thousand two hundred fifty pounds fire-and-forget weapon had a range of ninety miles and carried a warhead the weighed three hundred thirty pounds.

The F-35I's took off from Nevatim Air Force Base in southern Israel, referred to within the Israeli military as Air Force Base 28, and turned to a heading of three-six-zero or due north. Seventy-five miles later, they were cleared by the tower for a touch-and-go on runway 30 at Ben Gurion Airport in Tel Aviv. Pilots frequently used this maneuver to practice landing and familiarize themselves with the approach to a particular airport while not bringing the aircraft to a complete stop. When the Lightning II aircraft were two miles from touchdown, the tower cleared two civilian Gulfstream 350 aircraft for takeoff. They roared down runway 30 and lifted off just before the F-35I's did their touch-and-go's.

The switch took place at five hundred feet with the help of air traffic controllers, who were accustomed to working with the military on covert operations. The two G350's turned to a heading that would look on radar as if they were the F-35I's returning to Nevatim Air Force Base. Meanwhile, the two Lightning II aircraft took over the Gulfstream's IFR flight plan to Salalah, Oman. Each pilot put in the transponder code the tower gave the G350 aircraft and adjusted their throttle setting to the cruise speed expected of a Gulfstream. On radar, there was no difference between the Lightning II aircraft and the Gulfstreams.

Everything went smoothly. As they approached the coast of Oman and began their descent, the pilots terminated their IFR flight plans and told the tower they were going VFR in uncontrolled airspace to sightsee—which meant they were responsible for their safety. The tower, glad to be free from monitoring the aircraft on a busy day, approved their request. On their own, the F-35I's descended to two hundred feet above the ocean, an altitude below Yemeni radar, and headed straight for the platform.

Approaching their target from the south, they saw the massive platform from a distance of several miles, seeing as they got closer that a large ship was docked at its base.

"That's an odd ship," one pilot commented, looking at the profile of the vessel. "I wonder what's under the four domes on its deck."

"It doesn't matter. If it's here, it belongs to the terrorists. I'll put one Rampage into it and the other into the platform. You put two into the platform. Three missiles should be enough to topple it."

Had the pilots not been making a low-level approach from the south, they would have seen *LNG* painted in giant white letters on the hull. The liquified natural gas carrier held thirty-three million gallons of LNG, the equivalent of twenty billion gallons of natural gas.

The F-35I's were traveling at a high rate of speed to avoid being detected by anyone on the platform. One mile from the target, which was approximately five seconds at their airspeed, they released the missiles, pulled back on their power, and banked hard away from the platform. That maneuver saved their lives because a hellish inferno vaporized the ship and platform when the Rampage missile struck the LNG vessel. The aircraft would also have been vaporized had they continued on course and not banked. Instead, because they turned to photograph the damage, they survived.

Both pilots thought nothing about the enormity of the blast, believing the detonation of the missile fuel caused the explosion on the ship. Feeling good about what happened, they gave themselves high fives after landing at Nevatim Air Base and were smoking a victory cigar when they entered base operations. Thirty minutes later, that bravado was gone. The cigars were in the trash, and they were braced at attention in front of their commanding officer's desk, learning about the shit storm they unwittingly created. Although the squadron commander knew it wasn't their fault, and he would have offloaded his weapons into the ship and platform if he were in their position, shit flowed downhill in the military, and he already had his ass chewed by his boss.

The calmest person in this fiasco was the minister of defense, who called the squadron commander and said that he and the pilots executed the mission to perfection and that it was his bad. The prime minister had the antithesis of that reaction, angrily phoning Talman and informing him that this was solely his debacle. Talman waited to respond, confused at what the prime minister was talking about, but knowing that finger-pointing was a requisite skill for holding political office in any country.

"What debacle?"

"The Yemeni government reported one of its LNG carriers exploded and took with it its country's principal pumping station."

"I don't understand?" Talman confessed, having been informed earlier by someone in the minister of defense's office that the mission was successful.

"Let me break this down into bite-sized pieces. The platform you photographed was a Yemeni LNG pumping station. Its existence wasn't public, probably because the government feared the Saudi government, or another regional adversary, would do what we did. The ship docked beside it was carrying liquified natural gas. It may have been pumping that gas to the platform, whose booster pumps would move it through the line extending to shore. So far, no one knows what caused the explosion and, given the platform and ship were vaporized, it will thankfully remain a mystery."

"That means the Hwasong missiles are still out there," Talman said in a worried voice.

"And if you don't find them, the ship and platform won't be all that's vaporized."

In a twist of irony, McInnes phoned Talman less than ten minutes after the director of Mossad finished his call with the prime minister, informing him of the sinking of the Abby Aurora and what the Global Hawk detected in its cargo hold.

"That happened hours ago. Why wasn't I informed until now?" Talman assertively asked.

"You're not part of the Department of Defense, Abe," McInnes countered in an irritable tone. "The intelligence I give you is out of professional courtesy."

"That cuts both ways."

"Understood. I know about the explosion off the coast of Yemen. It triggered an alert on one of our satellites. I have a recording if you'd like to see it," McInnes said, clearly taunting him.

"I hope your professional courtesy extends to misfiling it so that those within your government, particularly Congress, don't leak it to the press. I don't need one of our many adversaries using this against Israel in the future."

"It'll be director's eyes only and left out of the President's Daily Brief."

"Thank you."

"If I called you earlier on the sinking of the Abby Aurora, it wouldn't have altered your aircraft strike."

"Why is that?"

"Because the ship was sailing south, away from the Middle East. We suspect there may be up to three vessels delivering a duplicate shipment to that platform in the Arabian Sea."

"Do you know their locations?"

"Not yet." McInnes didn't want to discuss his drone situation.

"What do you know about these ships?"

McInnes provided their names and last known courses.

"They're sailing towards Yemen," Talman said with a sigh.

"That shouldn't come as a surprise. We knew the platform was in the Arabian Sea, and you just leveled a platform off Yemen."

"But now my hands are tied. The prime minister won't let me send a paper glider into that area until things calm down."

"You're not without resources, Abe. Are you good friends with the minister of defense?"

"I was, but now I'm not so sure. I made him look bad. Even if he agreed to send aircraft back into the Arabian Sea, the prime minister would override that decision. I can't send a warship; it would take too long."

"Think outside the box."

"What am I missing?"

McInnes told him.

CHAPTER 15

October 16, 2021—EMP devices arrive in Israel

An electromagnetic pulse, or EMP, is a wave of electromagnetic radiation that will destroy or severely damage anything which contains an electrical circuit or component. Power grids, broadcast stations, computers, vehicles, aircraft controls, cellular phones, generators, and anything else depending on even small amounts of electricity will fail when hit by the pulse. The good news: it's not harmful to humans or animals.

An explosively pumped flux compression generator, or EPFCG produces an extremely intense EMP, capable of producing tens of millions of amperes and tens of terawatts. This uses an explosive to compress the magnetic flux and generate a massive EMP, which can be funneled to a highly directional antenna that's pointed toward the target.

Major General Akbar Hassani had only secondhand knowledge of electromagnetic radiation, being told for years by military scientists that if Iran's enemies set off such a device inside the country, within its radius of effectiveness it would render every weapon more sophisticated than a revolver useless. He hadn't considered using it as an offensive weapon until recently because he preferred to physically destroy a target rather than render it inoperative. That changed in his plan to attack Israel, where an EMP device proved to be the perfect weapon to render the country vulnerable to an attack.

To effectively defeat the Jewish state, he needed to destroy the Israeli defense systems protecting the five cities he was targeting. According to his scientists, unless he neutralized their shields, there was a low probability that the twenty warheads would reach their targets. That would be a disaster because it would allow Israel to launch a nuclear retaliatory strike. Since their defensive systems weren't nearly as sophisticated as the Jewish state, he didn't think the military or his country's leadership would survive the attack. Therefore, the EMP detonations were crucial for the success of the operation and his country's survival.

The electromagnetic pulse devices constructed to take down Israeli defense shields weren't unobtrusive. By necessity, because of the enormous pulse they needed to produce, the devices were large—each measuring ten feet long, four feet high, three feet wide, and weighing two thousand six hundred sixty pounds. To hide their acutely suspicious appearance, they were placed within the steel housing of branded commercial backup generators and shipped without their explosive charge to get past the canines and explosive detection equipment at Israeli ports.

The five EMP devices began their journey from Tehran aboard a military cargo aircraft that transported them to Latakia, the principal port city of Syria. Taken off the aircraft and placed in two Syrian military cargo haulers, they were trucked to a lift netter commercial fishing trawler—a vessel that lowered large nets over the sides and used powerful lights to attract fish to the surface. Because the devices collectively weighed seven tons, the trawler was noticeably low in the water. Had it not left port several hours before the traditional time the other fishing boats departed, both the loading of the generators and the heaviness of the vessel would have been noticed and a subject of conversation between the captains of other ships.

Eighty-five miles from port, the trawler rendezvoused with three ships anchored in the Mediterranean Sea. The devices were lifted from the trawler and lowered into the holds of the three boats. Once the transfers were complete, they weighed anchor and set course for Israel, arriving in the early morning, as scheduled, at the ports of Haifa, Ashdod, and Eilat.

The ship that berthed in Haifa carried two EMP devices—one would remain in that city, and the other trucked to Tel Aviv, which was fifty-seven miles away. The second device onboard the Ashdod vessel would be transported to Jerusalem—a distance of fifty miles.

The pseudo generators cleared customs and, once the duty was paid, were picked up by agents of the Iranian government who years ago embedded themselves as merchants in local communities. Besides being spies, they were experts with explosives who instructed others in bomb-making. Because of the importance of what they were about to do, each agent was told to suspend training and refrain from covert activities.

The agent's expertise with explosives was critical. If the charge was a centimeter out of position or a gram off on the amount of explosive used, all that would happen would be shrapnel flying in every direction from the disintegrated generator frame. For the device to produce a pulse, a precise amount of explosive needed to be exactly positioned around a specific tube. If correctly done, the detonation would produce an implosion, compressing the magnetic flux and generating an EMP channeled through an antenna directed at an Israeli missile defense shield. A multi-directional antenna was used for Tel Aviv and Jerusalem, which had more than one shield. Each device was built to have a range of thirty miles, giving flexibility in their placement so that an effective EMP could impact the dispersed missile defense centers in these cities.

The five targeted cities were selected because their destruction would shatter the Israeli government, annihilate its strategic military capabilities, and immolate or kill from radiation poisoning one million eight hundred thousand people—twenty percent of the population. Those who survived but suffering from the effects of radiation, calculated to be in the hundreds of thousands, would require years of medical attention. This would place a tremendous burden on a defenseless government whose economy was now in tatters. It wouldn't take long for Israel to be subjugated into obscurity by its encroaching neighbors and those bent on destroying every vestige of the Jewish state—which was Iran's intent.

The five generators/EMP devices cleared customs without issue and were loaded by forklift into the trucks sent to retrieve them. The agents took it to their place of business, after which they wasted no time getting to work on the devices. Using the diagram, explosive, detonator, and cellular trigger each was messengered, they deftly prepared the EMT devices. This took two hours. Afterward, each agent made themselves comfortable and waited. They accepted the assignment knowing that success meant they'd either die in the EMP explosion or when the nuclear warhead exploded above their city. Satisfied with being martyrs, no one considered refusing the honor of giving their life in the service of Allah to destroy Israel.

The instructions Hassani sent required them to stay at their place of business until three-thirty a.m. the morning of the missile launch when they'd drive the device to its predetermined location. At that time, merchant truck deliveries were common and attracted little attention. There was no thought of parking the truck for longer than the anticipated one hour and forty-five minutes because that would be a red flag to the ever-vigilant police or the average Israeli who lived with the constant threat of bombings. Uncrewed trucks were always at the top of their list for hiding large explosive devices, while drivers remaining in their vehicles attracted less attention.

Hassani and his team considered getting the trucks into position fifteen to twenty minutes before detonation. However, the consensus was that if something went wrong—such as a vehicle having a flat tire or a maintenance issue, the extra hour would allow the agent to move the device to the backup truck. Since the launch time was fixed, the devices had to detonate on time. Therefore, they decided the trucks would move into position slightly less than two hours before the EMP devices exploded.

Emmet Manker held the Israeli naval rank of sgan-aluf, which translated to deputy champion and equated to the US navy rank of commander. He captained the seven hundred twenty million dollars Israeli Dolphin-class submarine Avenger—a diesel-electric craft built in Germany and put into service in 2017. The vessel was one hundred eighty-eight feet in length, with a beam of over twenty-two feet and a draught of slightly over twenty. The manufacturer certified it could descend to a depth of one thousand one hundred fifty feet and attain a speed of twenty-nine mph. Manker, who commanded the ship since its launch, never came close to testing that depth. However, he frequently pushed the engineering crew for increased speed and discovered the Avenger could do two mph beyond specs.

The Dolphin-class submarine carried an arsenal of six torpedoes and ten Popeye sea-launched cruise missiles, or SLCMs, which had a range of nine hundred thirty miles. Each could be fitted with one of the ten, two hundred kiloton nuclear warheads the Avenger carried. The minister of defense assigned this strategic weapon to the Arabian Sea, designating its patrol area as a triangle extending from the northern tip of Oman, east towards the coast of Pakistan, and southwest to the Gulf of Aden.

Talman requested the Avenger from the minister of defense after the director of the NSA suggested he use that submarine to search for the platform and the three ships headed for it, indicating it was the closest Israeli naval asset to the area in which the platform was believed to be located. Initially irritated that the NSA could pinpoint his submarines by name, the minister put that concern aside for a later discussion with his staff.

"If the Americans are right, and the platform and ships are in the areas they say, we need to put the defense of our country in our hands and not rely on another country," the minister said. "Even though we bombed the wrong platform, that doesn't mean the other doesn't exist."

Talman seemed stunned by that remark.

"Don't look surprised. Timidity equates to defeat in a conflict."

"How will the prime minister react to this decision?"

"After what happened off the coast of Yemen, the trust in both of us is, for the moment, gone. He'll want positive proof that we're going to hit the right platform or, if it comes down to it, destroy the ship that's carrying the missiles. He'll also want some measure of control."

"How will that work?"

"It won't. I'm not here to please politicians. I'm here to protect Israel. I don't mind being wrong a dozen times if it leads me to the answer. That said, make sure we get this one right. Based on what you and the NSA are saying, we won't have time for a re-do."

"The PM will fire us for not telling him. We'll lose our pensions."

"Is that a concern?"

"No."

"Good, because when he eventually reads the message I'm about to send to the sgan-aluf of the Avenger, it will send him over the edge."

Manker was in his cabin when he heard a knock at the door. He told the person to enter.

"An emergency action message," the communications officer said, extending a letter-size envelope with the legend *Top Secret* stamped in heavy red block print across the top.

Once the officer left, he opened the envelope and unfolded the single page message, which carried the same Top Secret legend. The heading and the printed signature at the bottom showed it was from the minister of defense.

The Avenger is to immediately proceed at the fastest possible speed from its current position to the southern edge of the Gulf of Aden at a point perpendicular to the land boundary between Oman and Yemen.

In that general area, you're to conduct an expeditious search for an oil platform serving as a missile launch site and for the Hao Chang, Bhari Ghazal, and Morning Sun—three ships *believed to be going to this platform. One or more of these vessels may be transporting missiles armed with nuclear warheads, which are to be launched at Israel. Destroy these vessels and the platform, without regard to casualties, if you detect strategic weapons.* The message provided the last known heading of each ship and ended with XP70U9T1, the authorization authenticator.

Protocol dictated the commander and their XO needed to confirm the authenticity of an emergency action message. Manker summoned his second in command to his cabin and, when he arrived, showed him the message. As he read it, Manker opened his safe and removed a folder containing a sealed red plastic card, referred to as a Sealed Authentication System or SAS, which had a perforation down the middle. Snapping it in half, he pulled out the paper slip and handed it to the XO, who held below the alphanumeric code at the end of the message. Both verified it was a match.

"Let's get to the bridge," Manker said after relocking his safe.

When they arrived, he ordered a course change to a southerly heading and an increase in speed to flank, the ship's maximum speed, which was in deference to full speed—the top speed declared by the manufacturer. This was ninety percent of flank so that the vessel's builder could contractually protect itself from the enhanced strain on the ship's systems and the increased rate of component failure that occurred at flank.

The executive officer was plotting the vessel's new course at the electronic chart display, and Manker joined him after changing the submarine's course and speed.

"The southern Gulf of Aden, perpendicular to the boundary of Oman and Yemen. The minister may think he's giving the location of the ships, but that area is so vast it's like trying to see three corks floating in the port of Haifa. Finding these ships will be a challenge," the XO said.

"Let's assume they maintain their present course. The corks will get closer to each other," Manker said, taking a grease pencil and drawing a small circle on the chart display.

"How do we detect missiles and warheads on these vessels if they're below deck? We can't sink any of these ships unless we confirm they're carrying strategic weapons."

"We'll follow them to the platform, which should be their convergent point. When they unload their cargo, we'll see what they're transporting. We must also consider the possibility these ships have underwater detection devices. Therefore, expect to run silent when we get close. If we're detected, they'll alter course and go their separate ways." Running silent meant shutting down nonessential systems and the crew refraining from making unnecessary sounds. It also necessitated they significantly reduce their speed to minimize propeller noise.

"At this speed, we're making as much noise as a brass band."

"That can't be helped. If we don't get to the southern gulf quickly, we'll lose them." Manker was lost in thought for thirty seconds as he stared at the electronic display. "The sea depth at the edge of the gulf is nine thousand feet. There's a thermocline along it," he added, pointing to the water temperatures on the chart. "We'll sail in the colder water. That will make us harder to detect."

The thermocline was a translation layer between deep and surface water in which the deeper water was significantly colder than the surface layer. The change in water density acted as a barrier, bending acoustic waves and shielding the submarine from view.

The smile on the XO's face showed he agreed.

"Set our depth at six hundred feet," Manker ordered.

CHAPTER 16

October 18, 2021—the Arabian Sea near the Yemeni island of Socotra

Wayan and Eka's escape never got past the planning stage. They intended to have Wayan pound on their compartment door and request they have a bathroom break. When it opened, and both guards followed procedure by entering to accompanying them down the passageway, they'd hit them with rusted steel tubes they'd twisted free from the bunk. Wayan and Eka would then tie them up with the bedding and calmly walk towards the bathroom. Since their presence in the middle of the night was not an unusual occurrence, the sentry at the end of the passageway would hopefully ask where their escorts were, allowing Wayan time to get close enough to hit him with the pipe he held behind his back. If they were still in the game at that point and not staring at the muzzle of the sentry's AK-47, they'd continue to the staircase where they again hoped to surprise the guard with the lack of an escort and render him unconscious. There was no disagreement between them that the plan depended on luck and guard incompetence to succeed. Given their situation, it was all they had.

As night approached, their ill-conceived plan went out the window, or porthole in this case, when the ship slowed to a stop and Cheup burst into their cabin. Accompanying him were the two

Alan Refkin

guards posted outside. They secured Wayan and Eka's wrists with flex cuffs and placed black hoods over their heads.

"What's going on?" Wayan asked, his voice muffled by the hood.

"I could ask you the same question," Cheup answered, looking at the missing supports on the bunk beds and seeing the rusted steel tubes lying on the floor.

Wayan and Eka didn't reply.

Cheup smiled. "You're temporarily leaving the ship and being taken somewhere which doesn't require eight of my crew to guard you around the clock. They have important duties to perform."

Wayan asked where they were. Cheup ignored the question and led the way out of the room, with the guards guiding Wayan and Eka to the main deck, across a steel ramp leading onto the platform, and up a series of steep stairs to the second deck. They then walked through a maze of corridors, their journey ending when they were shoved into a jail cell and their restraints and hoods removed.

"They smell. Once you can free some men, have them taken to a shower and given fresh clothes," Ock said.

Neither Wayan nor Eka knew the person talking with the captain or understood what was said because they spoke in Korean. However, because Cheup almost stood at attention when he faced him, and the stranger's tone was authoritative, there was little question he was in charge.

"It will be late tomorrow. My men will be busy erecting and securing the launch pads and assisting with the cabling and ducting," Cheup replied in Korean.

Ock approached the cell. "You don't know me," he said in broken English, "but I know a great deal about you. I'm responsible for your kidnapping and being here.

"Who are you?" Eka asked.

"Jae-Hwa Ock. I'm the deputy head of North Korea's secret police."

"That job must give you a great deal of satisfaction," Wayan said tauntingly.

"I get satisfaction from ridding my country of those who try to harm it and malcontents."

"That eliminates all but several hundred elitists in your government. Working for a murderous butcher wouldn't be my aspirational goal. It's not exactly a winner on a resume," Wayan said, again trying to taunt him.

"I only regret the supreme leader, and not I will be the one to question you in Pyongyang."

"It makes no difference to me which whack job asks the questions."

Ock, a pro at interrogation, ignored the taunts and focused on what he wanted to accomplish—which was getting them to worry about what would eventually happen and place the burden of guilt for the death of others squarely on their shoulders. In his experience, those interrogated became more cooperative and malleable, supplying information they wouldn't usually give on the spur-of-the-moment, when they had time to think about their situation. "I wonder if Captain Nabar knows you both are responsible for the death of the special forces soldiers who accompanied him on an exercise in the Indonesian jungle, the pilots that helped you and Melis Woo escape Macau, and even the death of his father."

Wayan and Eka were silent, although their expressions showed they were curious and had some measure of belief in what was said.

"Let me tell you why their blood is on your hands." Ock explained, going into detail on the deaths of the special forces team, Sehat Nabar, and the pilots of the aircraft who helped everyone escape Macau."

"Why kill Sehat Nabar?" Wayan added. "He was a harmless farmer."

"Farmer yes, harmless no. In an uncommon display of competence, the Indonesian military shot down our drone. Unfortunately, he recovered a piece of wreckage that identified the aircraft as North Korean. I couldn't let the police, or the press see it."

"The police didn't believe his story, and you took the piece of wreckage he had. The secret was already out when the Indonesian military recovered the remains of the drone. They knew the aircraft was North Korean. What did you gain by killing Sehat Nabar?"

"I got rid of a loose end. In my line of work, you never want to look over your shoulder. I couldn't afford the publicity if someone in the press later believed his story and decided to investigate. The Indonesian government wasn't a problem. Your country has a good relationship with us, and they want to maintain it. We have already settled for this unfortunate incident. In exchange for their silence, we're turning over a software technology that will increase the efficiency of your drones. That will save millions in research or licensing fees. We also promised to respect their sovereign territory in the future. They probably know we won't keep that promise, but it closed the chapter on this incident."

"The government didn't care about the lives of those you killed," Eka said, shaking her head.

"They realized there was nothing the dove could do when confronted with the hawk. They made the best of it."

"Who carried out Nabar's murder?" Wayan asked.

"An intelligence agent assigned to our Jakarta embassy." Ock stepped closer to the cell bars and looked Eka in the eyes. "I can't save your lives. The supreme leader wants to kill you, and nothing can prevent that from happening. However, if you tell me where Melis Woo is hiding or how to get back the money she stole, I promise you will have a quick death. Believe me when I say the alternative is horrific." Ock stepped away without another word and left.

Once he was gone, the Cheup looked at Wayan and Eka. "As you see, the bathroom is to your left and your bunks to the right. You'll receive your meals through this slot," he said, touching the rectangular-shaped opening in the cell bars. "Don't bother to call for anyone. The room your cell is in will be locked, and no one will be outside."

"You said we're temporarily leaving the ship. When will we return?" Eka asked.

"In two days."

"Then where?" Wayan asked.

"You already know the answer."

The Morning Sun was the first to arrive at the platform. Once the prisoners were escorted to their cell, the crew removed the five transporter-erector-launchers from the ship's cargo hold and placed them in specific spots on the main deck. It took four hours to level and secure them to the platform. An hour after the last securing screw was tightened, the Hao Chang docked.

Although the ship transporting the missiles was much larger than the Morning Sun, its holds were small because they were designed to carry earlier generation missiles and not the massive Hwasong-16. There was barely two feet of clearance as the platform crane slowly lifted the ICBMs out of the hold. The process was slow to avoid puncturing the weapons as they left the ship and were gently lowered onto the TELs secured to the main deck. It took eight hours to place the five missiles onto their launch pads. During this time, the Bahri Ghazal eased into its dock.

Ock, who Kim Jong-un charged with ensuring everything went smoothly, arrived before the first vessel docked. Getting him there was complicated because his name and face were in the databases of many of the world's intelligence agencies. Therefore, when he entered any of those countries, recognition software flagged him, and he was detained and questioned why he was there. When those questions were exhausted, they sent him packing. Fortunately, countries such as Indonesia, Yemen, and Australia didn't have him in their databases. Therefore, he could use a Chinese passport with an alias to enter a country without identifying himself as a North Korean. He took advantage of this passport to get to the platform, flying from Pyongyang to Shanghai and the Sana'a International Airport in Yemen. Taking a puddle jumper to the island of Socotra, one of his agents was waiting with a high-speed boat and brought him to the platform.

Ock was there to greet the captains of the first two vessels. However, the Bahri Ghazal was particularly important because, besides missile fuel and oxidizer, it transported a dignitary. Waiting on the dock, he watched the crew extend the boarding ramp. The first person off was Saeed Pasdar, Iran's minister of intelligence. The ayatollah's confidant was there for two reasons: to verify the delivery of the strategic weapons and press the button that launched the missiles. His journey, which was substantially shorter than those on the other vessels, took its toll on the septuagenarian—who was prone to seasickness and was white-faced and unsteady as he stepped off the ship ahead of his interpreter. After a brief greeting, Ock said he'd escort them to their quarters.

"Are you on schedule?" the minister asked. He was walking slowly with an unsteady gait.

"We are. Your technicians did an excellent job in preparing for our arrival."

Pasdar, who couldn't keep it together, rushed to the side of the platform and threw up. Fortunately, the wind was in his favor, and his last meal blew out to sea. "We'll speak later," he said.

After leading the minister and his interpreter to their rooms, Ock went to the main deck and watched as the last Hwasong-16 ICBM was lowered onto its launcher. Near it, the insulated fuel ducts were being connected to the other four missiles. With everything going smoothly, he took successive stairways until reaching the boat docks and walked onto the Hao Chang. Because the captain gave him a tour of the vessel after it docked, he knew where he was going and made his way to the third deck and entered the launch control center. The room was cramped with consoles, in front of which sat twenty technicians in white lab coats, who were focused on the digital displays on their LED screens that gave the status of the missiles' external and internal components and systems. Communication between the launch center and the missiles was through a wireless interface. If there was a problem, the Hao Chang carried spare parts to fix almost any malfunction.

Launch procedures dictated everyone be off the platform and onboard their ship at five-thirty a.m., thirty minutes before launch. At that time, the three vessels would cast off. The platform and Israel were in the same time zone. Tehran was thirty minutes ahead. Following the launch, Ock would return to North Korea with Wayan and Endah on the Hao Chang. If all went as planned, the most cataclysmic event in human history was slightly more than a day away.

CHAPTER 17

October 20, 2021—three-thirty a.m. in Israel, four-thirty a.m. on the platform

At *three-thirty a.m.*, the five trucks carrying the EMP devices exited warehouses in Haifa, Tel Aviv, Jerusalem, Ashdod, and Eilat. Each was driven to the top of a hill, the location of the trucks mathematically calculated by Iranian scientists using publicly available topographical maps of the Israeli cities and scouted by the agents ahead of time. The hill increased the range and potency of the weapon. Less ground interference meant a more powerful pulse when it penetrated the command and control structures and the defensive missiles they controlled.

In addition to the location where their vehicle was to be parked, each agent was given an antenna heading. The pulse they were generating had an operational range of thirty miles. However, considering the elevation of the hills and the building clutter between the device and the defense shields, the optimum distance from the device to the target was twelve miles—far enough away to not attract attention while maintaining maximum lethality.

The timetable called for the rear door of the trucks to be opened at five-forty a.m., five minutes before detonation. The agents had a choice of either staying with the vehicle and dying in the EMP blast or walking some distance away, watching the nuclear explosion, and being vaporized. The Hwasong-16's MIRVs, a quartet of four hundred seventy-five kiloton warheads, made each weapon twenty-six times more powerful than the atomic bomb dropped on Nagasaki. With that size detonation, the agents who walked away to view the explosion were told they might live to see a bright white light that rapidly changed to yellow before transforming to a fiery glowing orange mushroom. At the same time, fire clouds would form and disappear from the compression and expansion of the shock wave, which they wouldn't survive because the temperature at the center of that inferno was between fifty and one hundred fifty million degrees Fahrenheit. In comparison, the sun's temperature is twenty-seven million degrees at its core and ten million degrees Fahrenheit on its surface.

By four a.m., the five trucks were in place, and a circuitry test of the EMP devices showed they were functional. It was one hour and forty-five minutes until detonation.

Saeed Pasdar did not sleep well. Even though he was on a stable oil platform, water surrounded it. That thought lingered in his mind, and his bout of seasickness continued. Preferring an empty stomach, he ignored the fruit and other food in his room. Instead, he rolled out his prayer mat to perform the first of his five daily prayers, aligning it in the direction his interpreter told him was Mecca. Even though morning prayers began at sunrise, he asked Allah's forgiveness for being early because the launches were at that time.

Performing the cleaning ritual, he went to the sink and washed his face, head, hands, arms, and feet up to the ankles. Afterward, he began the Fajr, the first obligatory prayer, comprising two rakats—a series of recitations and movements.

"I intend to offer the Fajr prayer for Allah," Pasdar began as he raised his hands to his ears with his palms facing Mecca. He then stood, put his arms in front of him, his right hand on top of his left, and recited his prayers.

"Allahu Akbar," he said, bowing and placing his hands on

his knees. "Subhana rabbiya al azeem," he repeated three times in succession.

Standing up, he continued praying, "Samia Allah u liman hamidah, Rab'bana lakal hamid." He then knelt, pressed his palms and face to the floor, and continued with the chant "Allah Akbar." Sitting up and putting his hands on his thighs, he repeated "Allah Akbar" and placed his face and palms on the floor again. He repeated this sequence three times, completing the first rakat.

Following the second, which was essentially a duplicate of the first, he got dressed. He left the room and knocked on the door of the next compartment, finding his interpreter dressed and waiting. They started walking, believing it wouldn't be hard to find a stairway leading to the deck below so they could eventually descend to the level where the ships were docked. However, they quickly became lost and disoriented in the maze of corridors. Thankfully, they encountered a crewman who volunteered to escort them to the control room on the Hao Chang. Pasdar, who wasn't an advocate of exercise, became exhausted from ascending and descending the steep staircases. Still recovering from seasickness, he was out of breath and white as a sheet when he entered the control room.

Ock was standing behind a lab technician when the two Iranians entered an hour and a half before the scheduled launch. One look at Pasdar told him he wasn't well, and he handed him an unopened bottle of water that he grabbed off a console. After consuming half, the color returned to Pasdar's face. Ock directed him and the interpreter to two empty chairs in front of a console.

"Better?" Ock asked.

"Better," Pasdar confirmed. "Are we on schedule?"

"Yes. We've verified each missile is operational, and we're pumping fuel and oxidizer into them."

"How do I launch the ICBMs?" Pasdar asked, cutting to the chase.

"At six a.m., you'll lift the plastic cover and push this red button," Ock answered, pointing to it."

"Why is there only one button for five missiles?"

"If we launched them sequentially, our technicians believe the flames from the first missile would ignite the fuel and oxidizer in the other four. The thrust may also destabilize and topple the platform. Therefore, the five ICBMs will launch simultaneously."

Pasdar nodded in agreement.

"You said they're being fueled. Why wasn't that done earlier? Something could go wrong with that process. Our plan has no margin for error."

Ock explained the ICBMs needed an enormous amount of fuel and that it took some time to fill the five missiles because there was a single duct leading from the fuel storage tanks on the Bahri Ghazal to a junction box that parceled it to the five pumps which delivered the fuel to each missile. The same applied to the oxidizer. "Also, the fuel is very corrosive and can't remain in the missile for long," Ock added. "Fueling will be complete fifteen minutes before the ships disconnect from the platform. Forty-five minutes later, you'll press the button."

"Alhamd lilah rabiy alealamin," Pasdar responded, praising God, the lord of the worlds.

Wayan and Eka were lying on their cots, trying unsuccessfully to get some sleep, when Cheup and two crewmen carrying AK-47's entered the room.

"Stand up. I've been ordered to take you both for a shower. Afterward, you'll put these clothes on," Cheup said, holding what looked to be clothing he'd taken from the crew.

Wayan and Eka both stood. "You go first," Wayan said to her.

"Both of you will shower together, and my men will watch to ensure you don't try and escape."

"You're quite the gentleman," Eka said sarcastically.

Cheup ignored the remark and ordered a crewman to open the

cell door and put flex cuffs on them. Balancing the clothing in one hand, he removed the key from his pocket and handed it to him.

Everything that followed was a spur-of-the-moment decision by Wayan. The man who unlocked the cell door shouldered his weapon because he had flex cuffs in one hand and the key in the other. When the door opened, Cheup ordered Wayan and Eka to put their hands behind their backs, a command they followed. As the crewman put the key in his pocket and walked behind Wayan, the ex-police detective pivoted and elbowed him as hard as he could in the forehead. The vicious blow rendered the man unconscious, and he collapsed to the floor. When Eka saw her partner attack the crewman, she rushed out of the cell and pushed Cheup backward into the other crewman to give her partner time to react. Wayan took the cue; quickly stepping forward, he shoved Cheup aside and onto the floor before planting his fist in the crewman's jaw. The burly sailor was out for the count.

"Get back in your cell. You're going to get me killed," Cheup shrieked in Korean, although neither Wayan nor Eka understood what he said.

"I've had enough of you," Wayan responded. Bending over, he punched the captain in the face and knocked him out. "While I drag these two into the cell, tear the designer clothing he brought into seven or eight strips. We'll use it to tie and gag them."

Once the three were inside the cell, Wayan removed the key from the crewman's pocket and put it in his. Searching them, he threw their personal items outside the cell but kept the Satcom phone he found in Cheup's back pocket. When he touched the screen, a password box appeared. Wayan sighed in disappointment, knowing that the North Korean captain would rather die than give him the access code. He threw the phone against the wall in frustration, shattering it into a dozen pieces.

After Eka threw him the strips of clothing, he bound the crewmen with the flex cuffs meant for them, gagged the three, and used the remaining strips to bind Cheup and the legs of the crewmen.

"Should we take the automatic weapons?" Eka asked.

"Absolutely," Wayan answered, picking up an AK-47 and checking the magazine. After doing the same with the other weapon, he found neither was loaded. He showed an empty magazine to Eka.

"It looks like they didn't want us harmed. It would have been nice to know that earlier," Wayan said, dropping the weapon. "Let's get out of here."

Stepping into the corridor, Eka asked which way they should go.

"Since they put hoods over our heads and we don't know where we are, one direction is as good as the other."

Eka took off at a run to their left, and Wayan followed. Their goals were to get outside, establish where they'd been taken, and put as much distance between them and the North Koreans as possible before anyone could discover they'd escaped. That didn't happen. When they reached the end of the second corridor, they heard shouting behind them. Almost immediately, bullets ricocheted off the wall to Eka's left. Turning their heads to see who was shooting, they saw two North Koreans.

"I guess they didn't get the message that we get a pass," Wayan said as they tried to distance themselves from their pursuers.

In that statement, Wayan was entirely correct. Those shooting at them were from the Hao Chang and not the Morning Sun. They didn't know they shouldn't harm the prisoners. The crewmen were gathering their tools and equipment from the platform in preparation for departure and saw the escaped prisoners, who their captain told them about their first day on the platform. Therefore, the crewmen considered the escaped duo fair game.

CHAPTER 18

Ransomware is malware that encrypts files and demands a ransom for the decryption key. Without this mathematical key known only to the attacker, it's impossible to decrypt the files. Even if the data within the breached system is already encrypted, the ransomware will encrypt over it. The most common method for ransomware to enter a victim's computer is by masquerading as a trusted file. Once the victim opens it, the encryption process begins, and the user is locked out. The second way of inserting malware into a computer is to exploit security deficiencies in the system.

Melis Woo was very familiar with North Korea's central database in Pyongyang because she accessed it several times a day for years when laundering money for Kim Jong-un—each incursion requiring the unique passcode generated by a small fob-like device known as an RSA token. She planned to enter the central database again using the token she stole when she left the dictator's employ and pilfered his bank accounts.

Like that of most governments, the hermit kingdom's database was highly partitioned so that only those who had a need and clearance to obtain specific data could access it. The most sensitive area of the North Korean database was the executive section, which could only be accessed by Kim Jun-un and a small cadre of those he trusted with impunity. At one time, Woo was one of that cadre because she was the lynchpin for the country's money-laundering operations—whose current and historical information was stored in this section. She was now hoping to re-enter that section and write a program that would allow her to access this data in the future without an RSA passcode. However, this depended entirely on the supposition that the RSA token she stole was still active because she needed it to get her into the executive section to make her modifications.

Logic suggested the government had deactivated the code-generating token. The dictator issued three for his money-laundering activities. Kulon Sanadi, Woo's former boss, and General Min Kang had one, but they were dead. Kang's was in Beijing being used by his replacement, the money-laundering function moving there from Hong Kong when she absconded with the dictator's money and, unknown to everyone, his RSA token. The third token belonged to Kim Jong-un, who was issued one solely because it was his money-laundering operation. However, Sanadi and Kang knew the dictator had no idea how the token worked and probably put it in a drawer or safe and forgot about it. The minions on Kim Jong-un's staff weren't involved with the RSA tokens because he didn't want them to have access to this sensitive information. Therefore, since the dictator never used the token, Woo believed he'd forgotten about it and therefore wouldn't think about canceling Sanadi's. All this was good in theory. She was about to find out if her logic prevailed.

Woo began her hack by inserting the RSA token into her computer and generating a passcode that was good for sixty seconds. The one-minute limitation wasn't of consequence because she'd entered the system hundreds of times before and was familiar with the procedures. When the login screen asked for a code, she took a deep breath, typed the passcode generated by the token, and pressed the enter key. A split second later, she was inside the executive section.

Taking the fob that contained the program she wrote, she put it into a USB port and touched the enter key. Thirty-five seconds later, not only did the North Korean government no longer have access to its money, but it also couldn't communicate with its missiles— or get rocket data, nuclear research, military plans, the names of covert agents and spies, or anything else. It was now Woo's system, and anyone who wanted to get in needed the decrypt key from her.

October 20, 2021—ten-forty a.m. in Pyongyang, four-forty a.m. on the platform

Ten gunshots echoed throughout the underground office complex beneath the presidential compound at Ryongsong. The victim was the now-former head of Kim Jong-un's IT security. The genesis for his death was the message on the dictator's computer screen. It appeared in yellow letters against a pale green background within a rectangular, red-bordered box.

I control your computer system, and everything within it is encrypted with an algorithm and a unique key. Online backups and mirror files have been overwritten, and recovery tools have been rendered inactive. Without my electronic key, you can't access your data.

You have one hour to prove to me that Gunter Wayan and Eka Endah are alive and well. My program contains a timer that, upon expiration, triggers a subroutine that deletes your system's ability to accept the decryption key. With luck, you may be able to decrypt and access your files in half a century—once quantum computers become mainstream.

Send a video of Wayan and Endah to the internet address at the end of this message. Have them speak and give their dates of birth so that I know the video is current. I've inserted undetectable codes into hundreds of locations within your system, allowing me to access and encrypt your data at my pleasure in the future to ensure you won't attack them again. Trust me; you won't find them all. If any harm comes to either of them, you're responsible. If they die in an aircraft explosion, suffer a heart attack, are killed in a traffic accident, succumb to the flu, or die of anything other than old age, you'll suffer the consequences. If you stay away from them, I'll stay out of your computer system—that's our arrangement.

Once you send the video, transport them to Bali. When they arrive, I'll send a command to decrypt your data. Again, you have an hour to prove to me they're alive and well. Break our arrangement, and you'll regret it. Melis Woo. An internet address followed.

October 20, 2021, @ eleven a.m. in Pyongyang, five a.m. on the platform

Ock got up from his chair and told Pasdar that he was conducting a final visual inspection. The Iranian, who didn't seem to care, imperiously moved his wrist in acknowledgment after his interpreter relayed that information. The deputy head of the North Korean secret police left the ship and headed to the main deck. He was on the staircase two decks below it when he heard gunfire.

His first thought was they were under attack by a special forces team. However, he didn't see a raft or other craft tied to the lower deck of the platform when he left the Hao Chang. He also believed a special forces team would use silencers to maintain the element of surprise. Those aroused his suspicion as to the cause of the gunfire. Once he eliminated a military incursion, the only other possibility that made sense was that his hostages escaped and were being shot at by one or more of the crew. That posed two unacceptable problems: they might try and disable or destroy the missiles, which they could do by interfering with their fueling, and they might be killed. Additionally, if Pasdar discovered the two hostages he was transporting escaped and interfered with the launch, not only would his government lose payment for the missiles and other hardware, but Iran would look for another weapons broker—probably Russia or China. He heard more gunshots.

Unarmed, he decided to get a weapon in the event he needed to kill one or more of the crew to protect the captives. He didn't want to pull security from the control room because he feared Pasdar would find out. He also wanted to avoid a shootout because of the distinct possibility the captives would be killed. Therefore, he decided to handle the situation, whatever it turned out to be, himself.

The closest cache of weapons for Ock was in the Hao Chang's armory, which was on the first deck and to the right as one stepped from the boarding ramp onto the ship. He didn't know what weaponry was inside because the captain only pointed to it and gave him the combination to the cipher lock when he toured the ship. When he entered, he saw that while the room was small, it housed over a hundred weapons. He looked for an AK-47 because it had decent stopping power. As he reached for one of a dozen that were neatly aligned in a row on a shelf, he saw a 12-gauge shotgun beside it. Re-thinking his decision on the AK-47, he decided the shotgun was the weapon he needed because it wouldn't send a high-velocity projectile into a missile or a fuel duct. Next to the shotgun were several boxes of ammunition. He grabbed the gun, loaded it, and stuffed extra ammo inside his pants pockets.

Returning to the platform, he was surprised to see the private investigators standing beside the Bahri Ghazal, forty yards away. Both had their backs to him. As he quietly approached, he heard them discussing how to destroy the missiles—something he couldn't allow to happen.

"We break the glass, take a flare gun," Wayan said, pointing to a pair in a steel box affixed to a support beam, "and send the flare into a fuel duct. The fire will ignite the fuel and the missiles. Boom."

"We'll be in the center of that boom because the fuel ship behind us will explode," Endah countered.

"Not if we cut off the fuel at the circular junction boxes and ignite one of the fuel ducts on the other side of it. I'll wrap my jacket around my hands. The vapor coming from the ice encrusting the cutoff wheel looks cold enough to give me frostbite and pull the skin off."

"It would," Ock confirmed.

Startled, Wayan and Endah turned around.

"That's an excellent plan. The missiles are fueled with liquid hydrogen, which leaves this ship at minus four hundred twenty-three degrees Fahrenheit," Ock said, nodding toward the Iranian vessel. "The other conduit is delivering liquid oxygen, which is the oxidizer. It's at minus two hundred ninety-eight degrees Fahrenheit. Touching either of the cutoff wheels on the junction boxes with your bare skin would give you frostbite and a serious burn."

"I guess it's time to return to our cabin," Wayan said, raising his hands. Eka also put her hands in the air.

"Unfortunately, that's not an option," Ock replied as he raised the shotgun to eye-level and fired twice in rapid succession.

The force of the blasts hurled Wayan and Eka backward. They landed hard and were motionless on the metal deck.

Ock walked to the bodies and kicked them to ensure he didn't receive a response. As he did, the two crewmen who were chasing them approached. Seconds later, four others joined them—two carrying handguns and the others armed with AK-47's. Ock shouldered his shotgun and walked to the two figures sprawled on the ground, bent down, and picked up the small yellow bags that were lying on the steel deck beside them. Each contained #9 shot. Although the bag's impact on the body was nonlethal, the trauma it caused rendered a person unconscious.

The satphone in Ock's inside jacket pocket vibrated. He removed it and extended the antenna. It was Kim Jong-un.

"Are the prisoners alive and well?" the dictator asked without preamble.

"They are," he replied, looking at the unconscious duo.

"I want a video of them sent to me within ten minutes. In it, both have to say their birthdates."

Questions from Kim Jun-un were a one-way street, meaning he was the one who asked the questions. Those who attempted to reverse that process were sent to a labor camp or became target practice for the dictator. As curious as Ock was about why he needed the video and a mention of the birthdates, he wasn't about to ask. "You'll have it," he said.

"Immediately after launch, put them in a boat, take them to the nearest airport, and accompany them to Bali. Call when you arrive." Their conversation ended in the usual manner— which meant without discussion.

Ock's heart raced, not knowing if he could accomplish either of the tasks given him. He had no idea if he could revive the pair and get them to say their birthdates within ten minutes, and neither had a passport or other form of identification because they were kidnapped in their sleeping attire. How was he going to get them on a commercial aircraft?

Looking at one of the platform supports, he saw a hose with a high-pressure nozzle attached to the end, used to wash the deck. He adjusted the nozzle to its lowest setting, turned the handle beside the hose, and sent a spray of saltwater onto Wayan and Endah's faces. It took ten seconds for them to regain consciousness and another ten to realize what was happening. As they coughed out the water they'd inhaled, they sat up. The six crewmen took up position near the escaped hostages and pointed their guns at them. Seeing the potential for disaster, Ock ordered them to lower their weapons and step back.

"Help them up," he ordered four of the crew.

Wayan and Endah were lifted to their feet. They were groggy and not the sharpest pencils in the pack. Once they could stand on their own, the crewmen moved away.

"Give me your birth dates," Ock said.

"What?" Wayan asked.

"Focus. I need each of you to say your birth dates," Ock repeated, turning on the satphone's video.

They did.

Looking at the recording, he saw their hair and faces were so wet they looked like they'd just gone swimming. In addition, their clothing was filthy, their posture slumped, and their expressions unfocused. With time running short, he had to go with it. He sent the video to Kim Jun-un, knowing he'd receive a call shortly. He wasn't disappointed. The conversation didn't go well. The dictator was irritated at the appearance of the captives because it showed they were treated in a less than hospitable manner. After chewing on Ock for half a minute, the dictator hung up.

Pulling aside the four crewmen who previously steadied Wayan and Eka, he told them to lock the escaped prisoners in a compartment aboard the Hao Chang, stay outside the room, and make sure they didn't escape. "Under no condition are they to be harmed," he continued. "If they are, you'll explain your actions to the supreme leader." No further clarification was needed. The four left with their prisoners.

Ock called Cheup's satphone, intending to tell him that he took charge of the prisoners. When the call went unanswered, he told the two remaining crewmen to search for him. "Start with the cells on the second level," he said. "Since the captives aren't there, they probably are. The ships depart in ten minutes. If you don't find him before then, leave him and get on board, or you'll be left behind." The crewmen took off at a run.

It was 5:20 a.m., ten minutes before the three ships were to leave the platform, twenty-five minutes prior to the detonation of the EMP devices, and forty minutes before launch.

CHAPTER 19

October 20, 2021—6:14 a.m. in *Tehran and 5:44 a.m. on the platform*

Tensions were high, and everyone was on edge as the supreme leader of Iran, his advisors, and Major General Hassani focused on the digital clock on the wall in front of them, watching the seconds tick away before the time changed to a quarter after the hour. They were less than a minute from detonating the EMP devices.

So far, everything went according to plan, Hassani receiving updates from the agents via Twitter that they were on schedule. Mindful that Israeli and western intelligence agencies had extraordinary intercept and analytical capabilities, the agents were given four keywords to memorize in a specific order. Therefore, even though the government's leadership was hunkered down in the Fordhow fuel enrichment plant, they were current on the agent's progress when the keywords appeared in their tweets, which could be on anything from the weather to the food in a local restaurant.

The first keyword indicated a truck was leaving the warehouse. The second meant they parked the vehicle on the hill. The third that the truck's rear doors were open. The one they'd just received a minute from detonation indicated there was no sign they'd been discovered.

Hassani stood in the center of the room. All eyes were laser-focused on the phone he held, which everyone knew contained the cell numbers of the five modified phones attached to the EMP devices. In less than sixty seconds, he'd call each in sequence. When the phone connected to the device received the incoming call, it converted the signal into an electrical current, setting off a small detonator charge. That triggered the primary explosive.

The major general stared at the digital clock, waiting for what seemed like an eternity for the second hand to sweep around it and advance the time to a quarter after the hour. When that moment came, and the clock displayed six-fifteen a.m., which was five forty-five a.m. on the platform and in Israel, he pressed the send key for the first number, after which he quickly called the remaining four.

The EMP detonations were loud and powerful, destroying the trucks and throwing shrapnel in every direction. The weapons performed as designed, the electromagnetic pulses rendering useless the urban defense centers and the defensive rings of missiles they controlled. In addition, the pulse fried the electrical circuitry in every electrical device within a dozen-mile radius. Five Israeli cities were now defenseless to a missile attack and unable to communicate their status with anyone.

The drivers were alive, at least for the moment, all having elected to leave their trucks, watch the fruits of their sacrifice, and die in the nuclear explosion.

The Bahri Ghazal, Morning Sun, and Hao Chang backed away from the platform at precisely five-thirty a.m. Cheup, and the three crewmen with him, were released from their cell and made it to their vessel as the bowlines were removed from the bollard. Ock was seated next to Pasdar. He, the Iranians, and everyone else in the control room were watching the digital clock, which in their estimation seemed to have slowed as they waited for it to display six a.m. Ten minutes before launch time, Pasdar received a call. The conversation lasted for five minutes.

"The Israeli defense shields are down, and I've authorized the remainder of your payment. The missiles now belong to the Islamic Republic of Iran. Since they're fueled, why can't I launch them now?"

The short answer was that there wasn't any reason to wait an extra five minutes. The fifteen-minute differential between detonating the EMP devices and launching the ICBMs provided a margin of error if there was an unforeseen issue they could rectify in a quarter of an hour. There weren't any.

"As you stated, the missiles belong to the Islamic Republic of Iran," Ock replied. "You're go for launch."

Unlike a solid-fueled rocket, which is ready to go at any time, liquid-fueled missiles require a precise sequence of events to occur before pushing the launch button. If a critical item on one of the checklists was overlooked, the ICBM wasn't getting off the launch pad or would malfunction in flight. Since the checklists were extensive, Ock's director of flight operations, who had extensive experience launching liquid-fueled missiles, ordered his technicians to start going through their checklists as soon as the missiles were fueled, the oxidizer tanks filled, and the ducts detached. Subsequently, they finished every checklist item eleven minutes before the scheduled launch. All that needed to be done to send the ICBMs to their targets was for Pasdar to push the red button.

Upon hearing he was clear to launch the five Hwasong-16's, Pasdar unhesitatingly lifted the cover and pressed the red button. On the viewing screen in front of him, and those spread throughout the control room, he saw billows of smoke and fire pour from the bottom of the missile's engines as they ignited.

The Avenger began decreasing speed ten miles from the area given in the classified message to Manker, who didn't have a clue what he'd encounter once the periscope punched through water, and he looked at the surrounding area. To lower his risk of acoustic detection, he ordered the vessel to run silent and make a slow ascent from six hundred feet to periscope depth, sixty feet. As the submarine penetrated the thermocline, the sonar operator informed him he heard three distinct twin-screw propeller sounds, meaning three boats were in the area. The operator put their bearing at three-six-zero, due north and directly in front of the bow.

When the periscope was raised, the Avenger was three miles from the center of the area where Manker was told the three vessels would converge. That projection was uncannily accurate because the three cargo ships he was looking for were in front of him, their names painted on the side. However, they were no longer his center of attention. Instead, he was focused on the oil platform behind them, which had five large missiles atop it. Each was venting gas, showing a launch was imminent. He let the XO and the weapons officer have a look.

"Battle stations," Manker said to his XO. That command was relayed throughout the ship, and a klaxon sounded signaling to everyone aboard to quit what they were doing, go to their action station, and prepare for combat.

The most common method of launching a missile from a submarine is using a steam cannon, where an explosive charge flash-vaporizes a tank of water and turns it into steam. The pressure from the expanding steam provides sufficient momentum to drive the missile from the launch tube and clear the surface of the water. Once out of the water, it's slowed by gravity and appears to hang motionless in the air for a moment before the rocket ignites. However, the Dolphin-class submarine Avenger didn't launch its Popeye SLCMs with a steam cannon. Instead, it sent them out one of ten torpedo tubes in the bow using a hydraulic system.

Manker withdrew the message he received earlier from the defense minister and shared with the XO, who was standing beside him. He read it loud enough for everyone on the bridge to hear.

"Your orders, sgan-aluf?" the XO asked.

"Target the platform with two Popeye missiles. Leave the three ships for now unless we confirm one or more are carrying strategic weapons or taking hostile action against us. If you detect either, put a torpedo into them," Manker answered.

The XO told the weapons officer, referred to as WEPS by officers aboard the submarine, to load the platform's coordinates into two SLCMs. He transferred the telemetry data to the missile's targeting computers within seconds. "Target entered, sir," WEPS said.

Hearing this, Manker returned to the periscope. In those few seconds, everything changed. He saw plumes of smoke and fire rolling off the sides of the platform, indicating that the missiles were being launched. "Fire! Fire the missiles now," he screamed at WEPS.

When Pasdar pressed the launch key, the fuel and oxidizer on each missile were pumped into a combustion chamber, where they were mixed and burned. This produced a high-temperature exhaust gas that went to a nozzle which accelerated its flow and created the missile's propulsion. Although each of the five Hwasong-16 engines and circuitry was manufactured by the same people in Facility Number One, their electrical and mechanical components were fractionally different, which meant a slight difference in the responsiveness and output power. Subsequently, two ICBMs lifted off the platform a tenth of a second before the other three.

The typical ICBM takes ten minutes to accelerate to four miles per second—the fastest it can go without its payload going into orbit. Liftoff speed is low because of the missile's weight and gravity. However, its speed increases logarithmically once momentum builds, and gravity becomes less of a factor. Manker saw the first two Hwasong-16's lift off in unison. Weighing three hundred and thirty thousand pounds each, they weren't setting any speed records for punching a hole in the sky. To the untrained eye, the remaining three left their launcher simultaneously. However, that tenth of a second differential made all the difference in the world because those missiles were still on the platform when the two Popeyes struck. The seven hundred and seventy-one pounds of high-explosive in each SLCM warhead destroyed the derelict platform in a maelstrom of fire and caused the three missiles to explode in a concussive firestorm. The platform, which was on life support after the two ICBMs launched, was blown apart and collapsed into the ocean.

When the liquid hydrogen fuel and oxidizer on the three missiles exploded, the turbulent firestorm spread in a circular pattern for hundreds of yards. The three vessels were anchored near the platform to get a good glimpse of the launch—the Hao Chang there for the additional reason of maintaining a solid wireless connection to effectuate the launch. Therefore, they were all within that fiery ring,

The exhaust temperature from a rocket launch is approximately five thousand eight hundred degrees Fahrenheit. The three exploding missiles and the munitions from the Popeye SLCMs significantly added to that temperature. Subsequently, when this wave of fire washed over the Bahri Ghazal, the Iranian vessel, returning with the unused liquid hydrogen and oxidizer, disappeared in a blinding flash. The Morning Sun, AKA the Ja Ryu, was unfortunately anchored close to that ship and suffered severe structural damage causing water to enter as if it were a sieve. While that would eventually sink it, the fiery explosions from the platform missiles accelerated it becoming a marine habitat.

The Hao Chang was several hundred yards from the Morning Sun, which protected it from the fiery debris and concussive force of the Iranian ship but not from the ring of fire from the exploding missiles. The boat caught fire from bow to stern, and there was no way for the crew to extinguish the growing inferno. The smoke was thick when the captain sounded the klaxon and used the intercom to give the command to abandon the ship. Everyone took off at a run for the lifeboats except for Ock, who remembered Kim Jong-un's orders and ran from his console seat to the compartment in which Wayan and Eka were being held. The four assigned guards had abandoned their stations. Without a key to enter their compartment, the only way in was to break the lock on the heavy door. He tried kicking it several times, but it held firm. With his eyes burning and coughing from the heavy smoke, he took a fire extinguisher off the wall and slammed it on the door handle several times, finally breaking it on his third try. Now that the lock was gone, he was able to push the door open.

"We have to get to the lifeboats," Ock said, looking at Wayan and Eka, who'd used bottled water to wet strips of sheeting and tie them over their nose and mouth.

Following him to the lifeboats, and with most of the ship engulfed in flames, they got into the last one just before it was lowered over the side. Although the Hao Chang might not sink because there was no exploding ammunition or anything else destructive enough to put a hole in the hull, it was an anchored piece of wreckage that would eventually become adrift when the heat separated the chain from the anchor.

"Where's the platform?" Wayan asked Ock. A moment later, they saw two enormous explosions in the distance.

"The platform is beneath us."

"How did that happen?"

"There's your answer," he said, pointing to the surfacing Dolphin-class sub.

CHAPTER 20

"Where did those come from?" McInnes asked, seeing two missiles slam into the platform. He and Parra were in his office looking at a live feed from one of the Predators that Goodburn secured from the CIA, and he was talking to the drone pilot who found the platform seconds before the SLCMs from the Avenger slammed into it. The second drone was in another search area.

"They looked like cruise missiles, but I only got a brief glimpse," the pilot said. "They didn't get the job done. Two ICBMs got airborne."

"What's the range of your missiles?" Parra asked.

"Seven miles."

"How far are the two missiles away from your drone?"

"Let me get a fix," the pilot said after he turned the drone toward the two missiles. He pushed the throttle to the stop and adjusted the attitude of his aircraft. "The Hellfire's laser guidance system shows they're three point one miles away and accelerating rapidly. I have a lock on one. I don't know if I have enough time to lock on the other."

"Lock onto them in sequence and fire your missiles now!" McInnes yelled.

The pilot immediately launched a Hellfire at the missile on which he was locked. The one hundred and four-pound missile, with a twenty-pound warhead, left the aircraft at nine hundred and ninety-five mph. He then banked the drone and locked on the second missile, which was at the fuzzy end of the maximum range the manufacturer gave the military, and fired a Hellfire at it. Following their progress on his LED screen, he watched for what seemed like an eternity.

The first Hellfire impacted the Hwasong-16 eighteen seconds after it left the drone; the second struck its target seven seconds later, the fiery red-orange explosions in two different areas of the sky looking like a fireworks display on steroids.

The Avenger surfaced and stopped several hundred yards from the dozen lifeboats clustered off the Hao Chang's stern, the ship engulfed in fire and billowing heavy clouds of black smoke. Manker, who was on a secure line with the defense minister, told him he destroyed three missiles, but two got away. He also said he sank two of the three ships referenced in his orders and that the third was burning.

The minister, who was told fifteen minutes ago that an EMP blast destroyed the missile shields protecting five major cities, now knew two ICBMs were going to impact defenseless areas of the country and kill tens of thousands of people—and there was nothing he could do to stop it. He was about to end his conversation with Manker to order an evacuation of those cities, hoping some lives would be saved, when his assistant told him he had an urgent call from Talman. He put Manker on hold, returning to their conversation several minutes later.

"Mossad informed me that an NSA drone destroyed those missiles. Israel is safe, at least for the time being. However, make no mistake. You and your crew saved thousands of lives today, aluf-mishne," the minister of defense said, telling Manker that he promoted him to the equivalent rank of a US navy captain.

"I'm just glad our people are safe," Manker responded, then thanked the minister for the promotion. "There's lifeboats in the water. What are my instructions?" he asked, getting back to the tasks at hand.

"Put them under guard and photograph the face of every person. I'll have the photos run through our facial recognition system." The minister provided the routing address where his communications officer was to send the digital photographs, and Manker wrote it down. "If there's anyone we want to question, you'll transport them to Israel as prisoners."

"What about those remaining behind?"

"I'll arrange for an anonymous call to the Yemeni government informing them of the lifeboats, providing your present coordinates so search and rescue will have no trouble finding them. Tell your crew to speak English when you take the photos. With luck, the survivors will think the submarine is American."

The raft from the Avenger carried five crewmembers—an officer with a holstered sidearm holding a digital camera and four enlisted with automatic weapons. They donned generic foul-weather gear to obscure their uniforms and wore no headgear. None of those in the lifeboats offered resistance. The officer, who held the Israeli naval rank of seren, equivalent to the US Navy rank of lieutenant, began photographing their faces. Afterward, he re-approached the two who didn't appear to be Korean or middle eastern, discovering they spoke English when he asked their names. Ock came forward and tried to prevent them from answering but fell silent when the officer withdrew his handgun, put it to his forehead, and said the next time he interfered, he'd be returned to wherever he was from in a body bag.

"Your accent isn't American," Ock said defiantly.

The officer pulled back the hammer on his gun and asked one of the crew for a body bag, several of which were visible in the corner of the raft.

Ock fell silent, and Wayan gave their names and said the person with the gun to their head had kidnapped them.

"Get on the raft. You can tell your story on the sub," the seren said. "You're safe with us."

Wayan and Eka didn't need a second invitation and boarded the raft with a helping hand from two of the sub's crew.

The officer took the gun away from Ock's head. "I'll return shortly," he said in a voice that was loud enough to be heard by those in the lifeboats. "Until then, don't leave the area. We will consider any lifeboat that does to have hostile intent and deal with the situation accordingly." After seeing what the officer did to Ock, no one doubted the outcome of that interpretation.

When Wayan and Eka entered the sub, it surprised them to see the flag of Israel on crewmember uniforms. Manker introduced himself and assigned them a compartment, the officers who resided there moving their gear and bunking with the crew. After they were given Israeli military clothing and allowed to clean up, the XO escorted them to the wardroom to get something to eat.

During this time, the defense ministry ran the photos taken by the officer through a facial recognition database. Saeed Pasdar, his interpreter, and Jae-Hwa Ock were red-flagged—the interpreter because he was known to attend meetings between the Iranian leadership and foreign dignitaries. Upon getting these results, the defense minister ordered Manker to bring them to Israel.

The officer and crewmen returned to the lifeboat, secured the three red-flagged individuals in flex cuffs, and took them on board the raft. Before leaving, the officer announced that Yemeni authorities were notified and would mount a rescue operation. "I'm told a rescue aircraft will fly over this area within an hour, and a ship will be here within three. You'll have to tough it out until then," he said.

They took the three hostages onboard the Avenger, brought them to the lowest deck, and chained them to steel grates. As they were being secured, the submarine submerged, set course for their home port, and again went below the thermocline. The Dolphin-class submarine avoided detection as it sailed the length of the Red Sea, passed through the Suez Canal, and surfaced in Israeli waters as it approached the Ashdod Naval Base.

Once the Avenger docked, six men in suits came on board. They placed the three prisoners in flex cuffs and put hoods over their heads. They were then taken to a waiting van and brought to a building in Tel Aviv, twenty-one miles from Ashdod. Talman was there to greet them and pulled the hoods from their heads. Ock and the interpreter had no idea who he was. Iran's Minister of Intelligence did and spat at him.

"Welcome to Tel Aviv, minister. We have much to discuss and all the time in the world to do it," Talman said.

Pasdar turned his back on him, a move duplicated by the interpreter.

"I think you need an attitude adjustment," Talman said before directing the small cadre of guards around the prisoners to escort them to separate solitary confinement cells in the basement, which had visual surveillance inside.

Wayan and Eka left the Avenger after the prisoners. They experienced the polar opposite of the hospitality given to the group that tried to send five ICBMs with nuclear warheads to destroy Israel. Taken to one of the twenty unique suites at the Norman, a fifty-room hotel in Tel Aviv, they exchanged their Israeli military attire for civilian clothing. They were then given an in-room massage and taken for a gourmet meal before their first debriefing.

The conversations with various people, who didn't identify themselves or their agency, took two days. On the third, they were told that Israel's Minister of Foreign Affairs spoke with his Indonesian counterpart, and they were leaving the hotel within the hour for the airport to board a flight to Bali. No passports were required.

Before they departed Tel Aviv, Wayan called Persik and provided their travel details. The flight was uneventful, and as they stepped off the plane, they were met by airport security and taken to the main terminal without passing through customs or immigration. Persik had called Tamala and Nabar. Therefore, the three greeted Wayan and Eka as they entered the terminal.

Eventually, Pasdar told Talman everything he wanted to know, although it took years. During this time, the now-former intelligence minister was kept in solitary confinement so that he couldn't speak with anyone and to break his defiant attitude. It worked. Once Talman wrung everything he could out of him, he was left alone and died of cancer three years after his last interrogation, refusing chemotherapy because he didn't want his life prolonged, and Talman wasn't going to argue the point. His interpreter, not believing his government would assume he didn't reveal any of the state secrets he'd learned in the numerous classified meetings he'd attended, which was a correct assumption as he gave up everything after only one month in captivity, refused to return to Iran. Instead, given a passport and money, he selected another country in which to live out his days in anonymity.

During his Israeli interrogation, Ock was between the proverbial rock and a hard place. He wasn't fanatically loyal to Kim Jong-un or even his job as deputy head of the secret service. He followed the orders of his superiors and did whatever they asked to get the perks that came with such loyalty. Going against the grain would have made him a resident of one of the labor camps or killed as an example to others.

He didn't have a problem telling the Mossad everything he knew about North Korea's global activities since he was looking out for himself. He wanted to act tough and eventually make a deal because he couldn't return home if freed. The dictator would never believe he didn't break under interrogation and become a double agent. Kim Jong-un would use him as an example, killing him in a grizzly manner to deter others from even considering betraying him.

"Tell us what you know, and we'll give you the same consideration as the Iranian interpreter," Talman said. "You've been here three months. How much I'm willing to accommodate you depends entirely on the value of the information I receive. I want a knowledge transfer. Once I get it, you're out of here within a week with money and a new identity."

Ock concluded his timing wasn't going to get better, and delaying giving useful intelligence to the Israeli would not get him anything more. "I'll give you what I know. Before I start, you must realize the supreme leader doesn't completely confide in anyone."

"Let's start with Scops Island."

"Facility Number One?"

"Yes."

"Now that it's been exposed, it's useless to North Korea. The United States will have a SIGINT and Keyhole satellites focused on it. With their sophistication, they can tell you how many ants are on the island and give you a transcript of their conversations."

Talman uncharacteristically laughed, believing he wasn't far off. "As I said, I want a knowledge transfer, including your involvement in the kidnapping of Gunter Wayan and Eka Endah. You went to a lot of trouble to kidnap two private investigators, and you're going to tell me why."

Ock took a deep breath and began to talk.

CHAPTER 21

October 20, 2021—7:30 a.m. in *Iran and 7 a.m. in Israel*

Major General Akbar Hassani came under intense criticism and second-guessing from the ayatollah and his advisors when it became apparent that none of the ICBMs impacted Israel. This was verified by the five LED screens, which displayed webcams from the targeted cities showing that everyday activities were normal.

"Why didn't the nuclear warheads strike Israel?" the ayatollah asked.

"I don't know," Hassani confessed.

That response wasn't comforting to the ayatollah, who chastised the major general for not knowing what happened because the Islamic State needed to prepare itself militarily and diplomatically for the consequences of this failure. That wasn't possible unless he knew what prevented the missiles from destroying Israel.

"The EMP devices detonated. My Israeli translators, who are in the next room, substantiated that when they tried unsuccessfully to call businesses in the areas where the defense shields were located. The previous day, they reached those businesses using phones that displayed no caller ID and spoke in Hebrew to whoever answered and apologized for dialing the wrong number. One minute after the scheduled EMP detonation, their calls to the same businesses didn't connect."

"Destroying the defense shields was an act of war. If Israel discovers we were behind the attack, there will be grave consequences."

"They can't trace the devices to us, and the cover stories for the agents are solid." "I don't need to remind you those stories have terminal cancer because the agents, who we expected to die, are alive because none stayed in their truck when their EMP device detonated. It will only be a matter of time until they're captured and interrogated."

Hassani knew the ayatollah was right. Even though there were no surveillance cameras on the hills where the trucks detonated, hundreds of them were on the streets leading there from the warehouses. The authorities would have a good idea of what they were looking for because large pieces of the truck would have survived. Although the agents were fiercely loyal to the Islamic State and would willingly die as martyrs, Israeli interrogators were the best in the world and would get from them everything they knew. Once Israel realized Iran was behind the attack, they'd launch aircraft, cruise missiles, and possibly nuclear weapons against his country.

"We need to kill the agents before the Israelis capture them," the ayatollah said, interrupting Hassani's train of thought.

"They'll martyr themselves if asked."

"I'll send the Quds," the ayatollah responded, ignoring the major general's suggestion they direct the agents to commit suicide. The Quds were an elite clandestine wing of the Islamic Revolutionary Guard Corps, who operated primarily on foreign soil. They answered only to the ayatollah and followed the supreme leader's orders without hesitation. Their past misdeeds included killing Iranian dissidents and destroying foreign middle eastern encampments. "Find out why Israel isn't incinerated—and what happened to minister Pasdar, the platform, the Bahri Ghazal, and my missiles. We know the ICBMs were fueled and within moments of launch because the minister authorized the transfer of funds to North Korea. Get me answers quickly." The ayatollah then turned to speak to the advisor on his right, ignoring Hassani and implying their discussion was over.

Returning to his makeshift office at the Fordhow fuel enrichment plant, Hassani needed a visual of what happened to the platform. Since he didn't have a spy satellite, the fastest way to get answers was to send an aircraft. A fighter didn't have the range and would require several refuelings. Therefore, he ordered a Boeing 707, which had a three thousand mile range and a top speed of around six hundred mph, to get him photographs. It reached the search area slightly less than three hours later. What he heard started a conga line of bad news when the pilot reported the platform was nowhere in sight and the only thing visible in the area was the smoldering hull of the Hao Chang—the charred name still visible on its side. Knowing this ship had the missile control center from which Pasdar would launch the ICBMs, Hassani felt nauseous. He assumed the Bahri Ghazal was also lost since he couldn't contact the captain, and one of the ships it was docked beside was a burned hulk. In less than a day, he'd lost five agents who provided invaluable intelligence on Israel; the minister of intelligence, who had unique relationships with a plethora of nefarious people and organizations; a pile of his country's cash, for which nothing was received; and a ruined reputation. He'd also infuriated a formidable enemy. Since he couldn't reach Ock, he assumed he had died on the Hao Chang. He didn't know how his death would affect his relationship with North Korea but figured their trust in him would be gone, and he'd have less latitude in future dealings with the rogue regime. Frustrated, he concluded the Israelis found out about the platform and destroyed it, the missiles, and the ships. He needed to find out how.

Hassani didn't have long to contemplate his failure. Sitting in his makeshift office not long after he told the ayatollah of the missing platform and burning ship, a Qud operative walked into his office and killed him without uttering a word.

The five Qud assassins entered Israel on United Arab Emirates passports accompanied by what appeared to be wives and families. The Israeli government has been trying to boost Arab tourism after the Abraham Accords normalized relations with several Arab countries, getting their message across on radio and social media that Israel wanted them to visit. Therefore, there was a noticeable increase in Arab tourists curious to see the land of their once bitter enemy.

Israeli border agents and those researching the identities of persons entering the country are the best in the world. To get past this scrutiny, a Qud member and their "family" lived together. They had a residence, valid driver's license, and other verifiable data from the country which issued their passport. Since the photos of the agent and their family were removed from every database in Iran, except for that exclusively used by the ayatollah, their true identities were only known to him and his immediate staff. Therefore, it was extremely difficult to pierce their covers.

Upon landing at the airport, the families took a taxi to their hotels. While the wife and children enjoyed the pool and other amenities, the assassins drove their rental cars and went to the agents' warehouses. None carried weapons because each was proficient in martial arts and taught to kill using everyday items.

The five Iranian agents who survived the EMP blast sent tweets to Hassani indirectly asking if they should leave the country because, if their covers weren't already blown, they would soon be, or should they commit one last act of terror in a suicide bombing? The major general responded by telling them to expect a visit from someone who would expedite their departure. The arrival of a visitor wasn't unusual because, whenever they required delivery of complex instructions, information too sensitive to be put in a call or tweet, documents, or materials, Hassani sent a messenger.

The five agents were killed, and their warehouses and residences were searched. Nothing incriminating Iran was found. Upon returning to the hotel, the Qud agents spent the next two days with their "families" to maintain their cover before returning to the UAE.

The Swedish embassy facilitated the video conference between Israel's minister of foreign affairs and his counterpart in North Korea in Pyongyang since the hermit kingdom didn't recognize Israel. Instead, it recognized the sovereignty of the State of Palestine over the Jewish State. Therefore, both governments needed an intermediary to communicate. The Swedish ambassador moderated the conversation once North Korea agreed to the call. He got an earful when Israel asked why North Korea was manufacturing ICBMs and MIRVs at Scops island, also called Facility Number One, and why these went to an Iranian-owned platform in the Arabian Sea, knowing they'd be launched at Israel. The North Korean minister angrily denied the accusations and declared them lies. A diplomatic pissing contest ensued, Israel's minister revealing some of the juicier details of Ock's debriefing. It wasn't long before Kim Jong-un jerked his minister out of his chair and took his place.

"What do you want for not spreading these lies?" the dictator asked.

"Legal possession of Scops Island."

Kim Jong-un thought for a moment, considering the pros and cons of losing the island. "It's of no further use to me. Take it, but I keep the equipment."

"The cost of rebuilding the five defense centers will be more than whatever's at Scops. We keep the equipment."

The dictator looked at the camera, conveying a murderous intent to the Israeli minister. "I'll personally ensure you won't be able to stop the next attack."

"There won't be a next time. The president of South Korea will be sitting in your chair before long, and you'll be a forgettable and sad footnote in history."

Kim Jong-un let out a string of expletives, which only the Swedish ambassador could understand but wouldn't repeat when later asked. The Israeli minister of foreign affairs and the Swedish ambassador watched as the dictator opened his drawer, took out a handgun, and emptied it into the camera, ending the call.

The plan to bring Ock to justice came from Nabar, who with

Tamala and Persik, greeted Wayan and Eka when they returned to Bali. After they entered the mansion, Persik opened a bottle of Champagne he'd purchased for the occasion, and everyone began to relax. Wayan and Eka took several hours telling what happened from the time they were kidnapped to the day they stepped onto the aircraft in Tel Aviv, with Persik filling them in on his request for Melis Woo's assistance, saying they'd probably be dead if she hadn't intervened. During their conversation, Wayan told Nabar that Ock ordered an intelligence agent assigned to the North Korean embassy in Jakarta to kill his father."

"What's their name?"

"I don't know. Talman promised the information and resources to take care of Ock and whoever helped him."

"I'm going to kill them."

"You might have to wait. Talman's only going to release Ock once he gets whatever useful intelligence he can wring from him."

"If he returns to North Korea, I'll never avenge his part in my father's death."

"Talman doesn't expect he'll return to North Korea. According to him, Kim Jong-un has a history of being risk-averse—killing former captives because he fears they've given their interrogator valuable intelligence or agreed to act as an agent for a foreign government," Wayan said.

"What's Ock's alternative?" Tamala asked.

"Talman gives him a ticket to the country of his choice."

"How do we find him?"

"Talman said he'd tell us."

"What's in it for him?" Nabar asked.

"He can't let Ock live because he knows Israel has Iran's minister of intelligence and is interrogating him. That's an international incident waiting to happen. Talman told us he would kill Ock once he was done with him but wouldn't mind if you did it because it allowed you to bring the person who ordered your father's death to justice. The same applies to the intelligence agent."

"And Mossad wouldn't be implicated in his murder, now or in the future," Nabar added.

"Talman knew it was an option you couldn't resist, although what he wanted was to take the risk from Mossad and put it on you if there was an investigation of Ock's death. I'm sure manipulating people toward a desired outcome is second nature to him," Wayan added.

"He's right; I won't pass on the opportunity. Let me know where Ock is, and I'll take it from there."

"You're not doing this on your own. We also want payback for what he did to us."

"I'm in," Persik said. "He was shooting at me too when he barged into the residence—but this has to be done right. He needs to disappear in such a way that there's no investigation and nothing leads back to us."

"You're right. Most of the perps we caught had a ready-fire-aim plan. But do we have anything better?" Wayan asked, throwing the question up for grabs

"As a matter of fact, I do," Persik answered.

CHAPTER 22

Three months later

Wayan received a visit from a well-dressed man of medium height and stature holding an attaché case. He didn't identify himself, only saying that Talman sent him. Wayan invited him inside the mansion and led him to his office, where Eka was going through her emails. She stopped when she saw the man enter.

"Mr. Talman asked me to give you this," the man said, removing a binder from his case and handing it to Wayan.

"I didn't get your name."

"Since I'm not going to give you my real name, does it matter?"

Wayan said it didn't, while Eka smiled—appreciating his honesty and directness.

Wayan opened the binder. The top page was a photocopy of a Turkish Airlines ticket, routing the traveler from Tel Aviv to Miami and continuing to Santa Cruz, Bolivia. The flight was five days from now. Behind it was a transcript of Ock's interrogation. Talman kept his word and provided the information he promised.

"I don't know the traveler," Wayan said, looking at the name on the ticket and passing the paper to Eka. "However, because he's in this binder, I assume it's Ock."

The man confirmed it was. "Director Talman said there was an agreement Captain Nabar would take care of this matter if provided the necessary information and resources. He sent me and the binder to honor this arrangement. You'll have to read the binder while I'm here and give it back to me."

"Wayan said he understood."

"I'm also to purchase airline tickets, make hotel reservations, and give you this," the man said, pulling a thick envelope from his case and handing it to Eka.

She looked inside and saw that it contained Bolivian bolivianos, their national currency.

"Give me your passports, and I'll issue the visas for Bolivia."

"How?" Eka asked.

"My problem, not yours."

"Five of us will go to Bolivia," Wayan said, giving him the additional names.

"I expected Captain Nabar, but not the others. No matter. I'll need personal information and their passports to issue them visas."

Wayan called Tamala, saying he and Nabar needed to take leave and come to Bali with their passports because it was time to implement Persik's plan. Tamala understood and said he'd speak with Nabar. His next call was to Persik, who replied that he'd be right over.

"Let me get started with the both of you. Passports?"

"You can do that here?" Eka asked.

"The man didn't answer. Instead, he removed two Bolivian visas from his attaché, which he'd previously completed, and affixed them to Wayan and Eka's passports. When Persik arrived, he took a small machine and a signed visa form from his case, filled it out, and attached it to his passport. He did the same for Tamala and Nabar when they arrived.

"Are these good?" Wayan questioned.

"Yours are. I'll activate the other three before the end of the day," he said. Let me get your flights and hotel rooms. The man did, booking them on an Avianca flight to Santa Cruz, Bolivia, the following morning. They would be staying at the Marriott.

The five arrived in Bolivia three days before Ock, giving them the time needed to implement Persik's plan. Although each had brown skin, they didn't look out of place in Bolivia because only five percent of the populace was white, two percent black, and the rest in between. They were in that grouping. Although none spoke Spanish, their English was good enough to get them what they needed, and they completed their preparations the evening before Ock's arrival.

The Turkish Airlines Boeing 787-9 left Ben Gurion airport in Tel Aviv at one a.m. and landed in Miami thirteen hours and fifty minutes later. Ock stretched his legs, got a bite to eat from the money Talman gave him, and boarded a Boeing 767 for Bolivia. He decided this was the best country to hide from Kim Jong-un and those he would hire to search for him. If he felt they were closing in, he could cross into Chile, Peru, Argentina, Brazil, or Paraguay. With the cost of living low, he'd live well off the cash Talman put onto a Visa debit card and the monthly subsidy he'd receive if he provided additional intelligence on North Korea. Since he only told Talman some of what he knew, he was confident the cash would flow for some time.

He landed at the Viru Viru International Airport in Santa Cruz, Bolivia, at eight p.m. and cleared customs and immigration without incident. He didn't notice the tall man sitting in a chair to the right as he exited customs and entered the main terminal. If Tamala were standing, he would have attracted his attention because he was thirteen inches taller than the average Bolivian male. However, Ock's attention was on finding a taxi and a hotel to spend the night. Therefore, he was looking for signs with the universal ground transport symbol.

Only Eka and Wayan knew him by sight. Therefore, to avoid losing him, Tamala initiated a FaceTime group call with the other team members and flipped the image so they could see everyone exiting customs. After looking at departing passengers for thirty minutes, Eka called out his name, and Persik took over.

When Ock left the terminal, he was confronted with two lines.

The longest was for taxis, where everyone had a pile of luggage with them—meaning it would take some time to figure out how to cram people and baggage into a size-challenged vehicle. The other line had only five well-heeled people in it waiting for one of the black SUVs to pull in front of them. Persik, dressed in a black suit and tie, waved Ock forward from the rear of the line and escorted him to an SUV beside the one in which a passenger's luggage was being loaded. Although this brought shouts and curses from the others who were waiting, it didn't bother the North Korean.

The driver of the SUV was Nabar, who Ock didn't recognize because he never saw a photo of him or Tamala. Since the jungle canopy in Sumbawa was so thick, and the drone's camera couldn't penetrate it, Ock knew ahead of time that he couldn't see anyone's face. Therefore, he decided to kill everyone taking part in the exercise using the drone's infrared sensors that detected body heat. That way, he would ensure that Tamala and Nabar would be among the casualties.

As the SUV left the airport, the North Korean leaned back in his seat. "Take me to an elegant hotel," he said in broken English to the driver—a muscular man with a thick torso who was wearing the traditional black suit and hat of a livery chauffeur.

"The Marriott or Radisson?" the driver asked in equally broken English.

"Is there nothing better?" Ock asked, feeling good because of the money he had, a stark contrast to his lifetime of being penniless and depending on the state for his livelihood and any luxuries thrown his way.

"Not here."

"Which hotel is closer?"

"The Marriott."

"I'm tired. Go there."

Ock didn't have luggage or personal items, figuring he'd get a toothbrush, comb, and whatever else he needed at the hotel or gut it out until he could go shopping in the morning.

The road they took wove through a line of wood-framed small businesses and homes. Two miles from the airport exit, the SUV turned onto a side road carved through the jungle. It was pitch black, with only the vehicle's lights piercing the darkness ahead of them.

"Where are we?"

"We're almost there."

Ock, who was leaning forward when he asked the question, again sat back.

The SUV stopped several hundred yards further down the road, and Nabar got out and opened the rear passenger door. Ock, believing this was a robbery, and knowing a bit of karate, got out and attacked the special forces officer. That was a mistake. After deflecting several lame karate moves, Nabar countered with a lightning-fast blow to the chest that took the North Korean's breath away and brought him to his knees. The ease with which he moved, and the strength of the impact, gave Ock the impression he was way out of his league in a fight. He took out his wallet and threw it at him. Nabar put it in his pocket.

Initially, he planned to give Ock a speech about the untold suffering and hardships he caused the families of the special forces soldiers that he'd killed. He'd then segue into the anguish he'd endured from the death of his father. Going over this monologue in his mind, he realized it was solely for his benefit. Nothing would bring those killed back from the dead, and Ock didn't give a flip about their deaths and never would. Casualties were meaningless to him as long as he attained his goal.

Once he made this determination, he struck with the speed of a cobra, and it was over in the blink of an eye. Nabar focused all his strength into the knuckle of his right hand and thrust it into the North Korean's sphenoid, also known as the wasp bone, which was in his temple. The force of the blow drove the pointed tips into the brain, killing him instantly.

Removing a small flashlight from his pocket, he frisked the corpse and found a passport and cellphone, stuffing them into his pockets. Hoisting the body into a fireman's carry, he carried it into the jungle and dumped Ock into the deep hole he'd dug the day before, the shovel still in the fresh dirt piled beside it. Smashing the cellphone into pieces and destroying the passport by setting it ablaze with a lighter, he threw the remnants of both on top of the body.

Nabar filled in the hole, which was deep enough not to have the scent of a decomposing body escape and attract animals. Wiping the shovel clean of his prints, he threw it into the jungle and walked back to his car. Thirty minutes later, the SUV was back in the parking lot from which he'd taken it after being wiped down and vacuumed to get rid of fingerprints and traces of dirt. Tamala, Wayan, Eka, and Persik were waiting in a vehicle outside the lot as Nabar put the vacuum into the trunk and got in.

"Everything okay?" Tamala asked.

"Half okay. He deserved to die for ordering my father's death. But he wasn't the one who killed him."

"You'll get that chance tomorrow when we get to Jakarta," Persik responded. "We leave in the morning."

The North Korean embassy in Jakarta was a gray-walled compound near the center of the city, guarded by Indonesian police on the outside and the North Korean military within. Apart from intelligence agents, those assigned there rarely left the compound. When they did, they were followed by the Badan Intelijen Negara, commonly referred to as BIN, the state intelligence agency. Man-Shik Yu was a major in the Korean People's Army and one of two intelligence agents assigned to the embassy. Because BIN always followed them, there was no chance of having a clandestine meeting with someone who could give them meaningful intelligence. Therefore, they decided to spy on Indonesia in another manner. Every day he and the other agent would get into their cars and drive to one of the seventeen military facilities in and around the city. They'd park in a public area, take photographs from inside the darkened windows of their vehicle, and listen to whatever conversations they could pick up—the antennas for their sensitive listening devices disguised as tubing for a bike rack that sat atop the vehicle.

Wayan learned about this after reading the transcript of Ock's interrogation.

"How do we know they're in the vehicles," Nabar asked Wayan.

"The ambassador only trusts the intelligence agents to leave the compound unescorted, and each has a vehicle. He's afraid anyone else might try to defect."

Wayan knew which car he was looking for because Ock explained during his interrogation that Indonesian diplomatic license plates were black against a white background. North Korea's plates began with the letters CD, followed by a two-digit embassy code and a serial number that denoted the person to whom the vehicle was assigned. Zero one would be the ambassador, zero three the senior intelligence agent, who was Yu, and zero four the captain working for him.

Nabar was in a vehicle near the compound when a black Honda Brio, a five-seat hatchback, left and entered the two-lane highway outside the embassy. The last two digits of the license number were zero three, indicating Yu was driving.

Additionally, according to Ock, they always parked in an available spot on the street. Since they weren't in a no parking zone or other restricted area, the government couldn't prohibit them from being there. That posed a problem for Nabar because the death of the intelligence agent was going to be witnessed by those in the government vehicle following them and anyone else who happened to be in the area. That meant escape would be difficult, if not impossible.

It was Persik who came up with a solution, although he credited the scriptwriter of a movie he'd recently seen. It called for Nabar and Tamala to steal a delivery van, go to their base, and retrieve items that only the military possessed. While they were doing this, the rest of the team would follow the government car trailing the Honda Brio and find out where Yu was going to park.

The North Korean intelligence officer drove to East Jakarta and parked across the street from Indonesian naval headquarters. The two agents in the government vehicle trailing the Honda selected a spot three cars behind Yu and shut off the engine. They'd followed him numerous times and knew he never left his car during his customary five-hour stint. In Ock's interrogation transcript, Wayan learned that all embassy intelligence officers electronically monitored and recorded cellphone calls, electronic transmissions, and person-to-person conversations within the targeted building for five hours. This was protocol because it was the maximum recording time for the hard drives within the sensors, and the intelligence officers wanted as much information as they could obtain.

Yu, and the intelligence officers before him, discovered where the senior officials' offices were, the location of labs with stringent security, the communications hub for a building or complex, and so forth. Subsequently, the position of the Honda was predetermined for every building, facility, or installation they monitored. If the officer couldn't park in the right spot, he'd move to the next intelligence target.

Tamala and Nabar arrived outside naval headquarters three and a half hours after Yu parked with Nabar at the wheel of the DHL truck. In a heavy cardboard box with it was the rocket recovered from the North Korean drone. Nabar wasn't an expert with explosives, but Tamala was. He'd taken the one hundred pound rocket from the base weapons bunker and converted it to an improvised explosive device. Creating the IED took only four components—a battery, a fuse, an explosive, and a switch. Once this was complete, he connected it to an electrical firing circuit synched to a two-way radio frequency used by special ops.

They pulled the DHL truck adjacent to Yu's Brio, took out the heavy cardboard box, and placed it behind the truck. After removing boxes at random and putting those beside it, they got back into the DHL truck and left. To the casual observer, it would appear they were looking for another parking space so they wouldn't be double-parked and snarl traffic. However, that belief only lasted until Tamala detonated the IED. The fiery explosion destroyed the Honda Brio and the two empty vehicles in front of it. The government car, shielded by other vehicles, was unscathed. When the government agents rushed to the demolished Honda, they saw Yu's charred and decapitated remains in the front seat.

Wirjawan's walled residence in Canggu was a fortress that the reclusive gangster seldom left. Because of the business he was in, the consensus among villagers and those who'd done business with him was that he had one or more escape routes from his house. Since it sat on a massive chunk of land atop a hill, the belief was that tunnels connected the residence to exits in the jungle. That assumption was correct. The two escape tunnels were wide enough for his ATVs, which he needed because he was in terrible shape and couldn't walk the length of either tunnel, which ended a hundred yards from his boat.

Paranoid about his safety, the rotund gangster was known to house his security team in his residence. Therefore, given this heavy security and the possibility of escape tunnels, they ruled out a frontal assault or breaking into his home. If they were going to kill him and Sueb, a different approach was needed. That came from Tamala.

"It's a long shot, but I can't see another way to get to them," the special forces major said. Everyone agreed with that assessment.

The day after the North Korean agent's demise, Tamala requested a meeting with Colonel Ganjar Durin. He was there to ask the air force colonel to do something that could end his career and get him incarcerated. Sitting in the colonel's office, he explained what he wanted and why.

"You want a government drone to put a missile into a private residence?" Durin asked, making sure he didn't misunderstand.

Tamala repeated what Wayan told him about his and Eka's kidnapping by Wirjawan and Sueb and that they were on their way to North Korea, where they would have been tortured and executed had they not been rescued. "Someone on that North Korean ship shot down the MALE drone."

"I'm still filling out paperwork on that incident. Major, everyone in Indonesia knows Wirjawan and his men are human traffickers and will do anything to make money. The problem is that no one can prove it or stay alive long enough to testify against him."

"It's only a matter of time until he goes after Gunter Wayan and Eka Endah again. The only way to ensure that doesn't happen is to kill him and the person who leads his mercenaries."

"The only way to ensure you kill the tumor is to cut it out."

Tamala had an idea of what that meant but wasn't sure.

"This discussion never happened. Instead, I summoned you here because I'm tasking you and Captain Nabar with helping me evaluate a CH-5 UAV the Chinese government is trying to sell us. It will be a live-fire exercise, and I'll be using the North Korean rocket recovered in Sumbawa for the weapon system portion of the evaluation."

Tamala cleared his throat and shook his head in the negative. "I believe we used that rocket in another test," he said.

"Would this test have something to do with the explosion outside naval headquarters and the death of a North Korean national?"

Tamala cleared his throat again, indirectly answering Durin's question.

"My mistake. I'll update the paperwork, and we'll use the laser-homing AR-2 missile instead."

"Who's the pilot?"

"I am. This is a highly secretive test, and I want to make sure only a small group knows about it. Give me the coordinates of Wirjawan's house to ensure I avoid it on this test."

"I'll get it. He lives Canggu."

"Canggu? That's over seven hundred miles from here."

"And past two of our offshore testing sites," Tamala said,

referring to restricted areas which prohibited marine and air traffic because of frequent military tests.

"Then no country will be spying on our evaluation flight," Durin replied. "What are the odds his house is near a newly designated drone test zone?"

It didn't take a rocket scientist to know what Durin was planning. "They'll be casualties. This could get you tossed out of the military and incarcerated."

"Cutting through the bullshit, isn't putting a missile up this guy's ass why you came to me?"

Tamala confessed it was, but now that the potential consequences of what he was asking moved from theory to reality, he didn't want to put him at risk. He said he'd find another way to neutralize Wirjawan and Sueb.

"The police won't be outraged that someone killed a house full of gangsters. They'll only go through the motions of an investigation because the deaths of Wirjawan and his gang will mean less crime and that people will be safer. They'll believe or want to believe that a rival gang put an RPG into the house. I don't think they'll suspect a drone strike."

"You're near the Denpasar airport. The controllers will see you on radar," Tamala said.

Durin thought for a moment before responding. "The drone is coming from Jakarta and will hug the sea to the target. Staying below two hundred feet, I'm undetectable on radar. If someone on a boat sees it, I'll say the drone was operating in a newly designated test zone they shouldn't have been in, and that maritime and airport authorities somehow didn't get that message or failed to put out the required warnings. Knowing government bureaucracy, that's an entirely believable statement."

Tamala said he appreciated the CYA and vowed their conversation would stay between them.

"It'd better, or I'm looking at my cellmate. Give me the

coordinates of the Canggu residence. I'll load it into the computer and erase it after the flight. When do you want to do this?"

"Late tomorrow night. Again, I appreciate you putting your ass on the line, colonel."

"These people are kotoran and leaches on our country. No tears will be shed by anyone."

Everyone was in Eka's Range Rover, which was parked to the side of the road and facing Wirjawan's well-lit residence in the distance. It was 10:58 p.m. The strike would happen in two minutes.

"The drone will come from the south," Tamala said, pointing in that direction. "We won't see it because it doesn't have navigation lights on its wingtips. It'll make a sharp one hundred eighty degree turn after firing the missile and return to the airbase in Jakarta."

Everyone's eyes alternated between looking at the car's digital clock display and the house, waiting for two minutes to pass. At precisely eleven p.m., without warning, Wirjawan's residence was demolished in a fiery explosion. One second it sat majestically at the top of the hill, with every interior and exterior light on to show off the size and elegance of the residence. The next, it was a bonfire with debris thrown half a mile in every direction. Wirjawan, Sueb, and the low-life's working for them perished in the blast.

CHAPTER 23

Three months after the local paper got a tip and ran an article about a rival gang sending an RPG into Wirjawan's residence, Wayan and Eka were back in their routine of getting up in the middle of the night and sitting on their patio for an hour or two before returning to bed. At 7 a.m., they were drinking Lavazza Perfetto Espresso Roast coffee on the patio when their doorbell rang. Wayan opened the door and saw it was Persik.

"You don't look happy to see me," the detective said, seeing the expression on Wayan's face. "I'm just here to have a cup of coffee with my friends."

Since he knew Persik didn't do anything without a purpose and wasn't exactly mister sociable, he wondered what he wanted. "The last time you showed up at this hour to have coffee with us, we were kidnapped that night and on our way to North Korea," Wayan said.

Persik didn't respond. He followed Wayan into the kitchen, where the private investigator fixed him a cup of coffee. As they walked onto the patio, Eka gave the detective a look that asked: *what do you want?*

"What? Can't a friend stop by for a cup of coffee?" Persik asked before kissing Eka on the cheek.

"You look nervous for someone who just came for coffee," Eka said.

Wayan sat to the left of Eka at the four-chair circular patio table, and Persik took the chair across from him.

"Is that any way to speak to someone who just got you a paying client?"

"Who's the client?" Eka asked in a suspicious voice.

"The Ministry of Defense."

"How are you involved with the ministry? Better yet, why do they want the services of two private investigators when they control the military, have access to the ministry of justice and government agencies I've probably never heard of?"

"First off, they don't care about me; they want the both of you. They were afraid to approach you directly given their lack of response to rescuing you after you'd been kidnapped. Knowing we're friends, they asked me to set a meeting. They have an assignment for W&E Investigations."

"What assignment?"

"They wouldn't tell me."

"When's the meeting?"

The doorbell rang.

"Right on time," Persik said, looking at his watch. He got up from his chair and went to the front door, returning with a stout person in his mid-fifties, five feet eight inches in height, with hickory-colored skin and short salt and pepper hair. He wore khaki pants and a short-sleeved blue shirt. "This is Defense Minister David Sondoro."

"No need for an introduction; I've seen you numerous times on the news," Wayan replied, getting up and shaking his hand. Eka did the same.

Sitting in the empty chair next to Persik, Sondoro apologized for the intrigue of the meeting.

"Let me get right to it. This is Dr. Fedir Kuzma," he began, taking a piece of paper from his jacket pocket and unfolding a grainy photo. "He's a Ukrainian scientist, formerly with the National Academy of Sciences, who was taken from his lab and forced to work against his will in a secret facility in Moscow. He's cooperating with the Russians because the Federal Security Service, or FSB, grabbed his wife from their house, and they're keeping her in a remote location. They made it clear she won't be released until he finishes his research."

"What research?" Wayan asked.

"Active camouflage technology. That makes something invisible at the touch of a button. He's the father of this technology, and every nation who's working on this built their systems based on his research before the Russians brought him to Moscow and closed that curtain."

"Can you explain how something becomes invisible?" Eka asked.

"Invisible means it's unable to be seen, not that it doesn't exist. His technology blends what's to be obscured into the surroundings so that optical sensors, surveillance cameras, and other detection systems don't know it's there. Imagine a row of tanks on a battlefield able to sneak up on an enemy position or a person walking undetected into a room and listening to a conversation."

"It's hard to believe other countries don't have something similar," Eka said.

"They do. However, their Achilles' heel is motion, which significantly weakens concealment. That's the wall no one has gotten past. Kuzma believes he'd found a way."

"How are you involved? While you're at it, explain why you want us," Wayan said.

"I want you because you're nobodies."

"Ouch. Thanks for the ego boost. Why are you here?"

"Because Dr. Kuzma wants to defect to Indonesia. I need you both to make that happen."

"Let's step back. How do you know so much about this scientist, his research, and his wife being held by the FSB if the Russians have him in a secret lab in Moscow?"

"The lab is across the street from our embassy. According to Dr. Kuzma, he saw someone from the embassy leave at noon every day and go to a restaurant next to it. One day, he went into that restaurant, bought a cup of coffee, and dropped a note on the floor beside the embassy employee. Contact was established."

"Why does someone with his knowledge want to defect here? Why not the United States, France, or Great Britain? They can stand up to Russia when they learn about the defection, which they eventually will. No disrespect, Indonesia can't."

"He's seen pictures of Bali and wants to relocate, as he put it, to the Garden of Eden. If I went through Ukrainian and Russian winters, I'd probably want to live somewhere tropical as well."

"What about his wife?"

"You'll also have to get her out. He won't defect without her. The good news is that she told him where she is."

"Where?"

"Oymyakon?"

"Is that in Russia?"

"It's a village of four hundred sixty-two in eastern Siberia and the coldest inhabited place in the world. She lives in a small house with someone in the village keeping an eye on her to ensure she's in good health and has enough firewood and supplies. She and her husband regularly speak, so we'll know if she's moved."

"It's winter. What's the temperature?"

"I looked that up. The high yesterday was minus thirty-two degrees Fahrenheit, and the low minus fifty-three. The good news is that everyone will be indoors."

"The bad is that visitors will stand out."

The defense minister was silent and broke off eye contact with Wayan.

"We'll be followed as soon as we leave the airport. An FSB agent is probably there seeing who's arriving and who's leaving," Eka said.

"Oymyakon doesn't have an airport. The closest one is five hundred sixty miles away. You'll drive from there and have a good cover story for visiting the village."

"And you want the nobodies because…?" Eka asked.

"I know what you did in shutting down the North Korean

money-laundering center in Hong Kong and, with the help of your friends, doing some amazing things in Bolivia, North Korea, the Arabian Sea, and so forth. I've known Suton for years. When I asked him if he knew of someone who could accomplish the impossible and wouldn't bring up a red flag when they entered Russia, he gave me your names, along with that of Major Tamala and Captain Nabar."

"I'll fix myself another coffee," Persik said, getting up from the table.

"Is he coming with the four of us?" Wayan asked, pointing to the detective and stopping him in his tracks.

"It's a bad idea to break up a team."

Persik sat back down.

"You mentioned a cover story," Wayan said.

"You'll be tourists and winter enthusiasts. That tour will include Moscow and Northern Russia. A travel agency in Jakarta, which has provided discrete services for us in the past, will arrange it. They'll get your visas from the Russian embassy."

"Indonesians aren't winter enthusiasts. We put on a sweater if the temperature dips below seventy degrees."

"It's the only cover story my team could think of to get everyone into Russia."

"I don't doubt we can get in, but how do we get Dr. Kuzma and his wife out of the country?"

"We're working on that?"

"Any ideas?" Wayan asked.

"Not yet. However, there is one more thing I neglected to mention. The Russians are building Dr. Kuzma a lab on a military base outside Moscow, and they'll complete it in two weeks. Once he's there, even the Americans couldn't get to him."

"You need James Bond, not us."

"He's not a nobody."

"Who do we contact if we need help when we're in-country?" Eka asked.

"You'll have the names and numbers of someone in our Moscow embassy and the consulate in St. Petersburg. When you call, identify yourself and complain about the tour. They'll come to a prearranged meeting place."

"Reading between the lines, if the Russians catch us with the doctor and his wife, the Indonesian government will deny any involvement," Wayan said.

"Count on it."

AUTHOR'S NOTES

This is a work of fiction, and the characters within are not meant to depict nor implicate anyone in the actual world. Moreover, representations of corruption, illegal activities, and actions taken by local and national governments and officials were made for the sake of the storyline. They didn't represent the past or current situation of those institutions. Substantial portions of *The Arrangement*, as stated below, are factual.

The prologue concluded with Wayan and Eka presumed dead—their eyes open in what the reader would later discover was a state of unconsciousness. In researching situations where individuals appeared to be dead but were found to have a heartbeat, I learned it's possible to have one's eyes open during unconsciousness. Therefore, I used this to create the presumption of death.

As far as I know, there are no abandoned or decommissioned oil platforms off Socotra, Yemen. One was placed there for the sake of the storyline to get the Hwasong-16 missiles within range of Israeli cities, yet far enough from the coast so that setting them atop the platform would go unnoticed by boats near shore. The platform's dimensions were taken from Hyundai Heavy Industry's Ocean Greatwhite rig, the world's largest semi-submersible drilling rig. Its interior was modified for the sake of the storyline. Further information on this enormous drilling facility can be obtained by visiting: (https://www.offshore-mag.com/drilling-completion/article/16770103/

hyundai-delivers-worlds-largest-semisubmersible-drilling-rig#:~:text=ULSAN,%20South%20Korea%20–%20Hyundai%20Heavy%20Industries%20(HHI),ft)%20long%20and%2078%20m%20(256%20ft)%20wide).

During my research, I discovered that the terms "platform" and "rig" are sometimes used interchangeably when referring to offshore structures. However, there's a difference. Rigs are mobile and are designed to drill and service wells. A platform is a structure permanently installed at a location to support wells. I sometimes used these interchangeably in the storyline to avoid the repetition of the word platform—Mea culpa.

I was surprised to learn that when the government issues the license for a platform, it doesn't let the company abandon it once the oil is depleted, at which point the platform is referred to within the industry as idle iron. While it's in use, the owner is responsible for annually filing a plan on how they intend to remove or dispose of the idle iron. The removal cost runs into the millions and is factored into the oil company's economic plan before obtaining the lease. Usually, idle iron is towed to a specific area of the ocean and sunk to form an artificial reef. Because of the high removal cost, decommissioned platforms can be purchased for pennies; the buyer subsequently assumes the removal cost from the owner. Platform maintenance is expensive. Saltwater corrosion, biological matter accumulation, and structural metal fatigue are just a few of the maintenance issues associated with offshore oil platforms, which have an average life of thirty to forty years.

I modified the procedures for fueling missiles because putting every step of that process into the manuscript would have significantly bogged the reader down in minutia. Therefore, I summarized the basics. Liberties were taken in describing the LH2 and LOX tubing. The junction boxes were inserted for the storyline. More information on rocket chemistry can be found in the April 15, 2016, NASA article by Beverly Perry at

(https://blogs.nasa.gov/Rocketology/tag/liquid-oxygen/). A June

4, 2000, article appearing in American Federation of Scientists, created by John Pike, and maintained by Steven Aftergood, provides an excellent description of ballistic missile basics. This can be found at (https://fas.org/nuke/intro/missile/basics.htm).

Flare guns carry a pyrotechnic payload. When shot at a person, it has negligible penetrating power. The risk of being struck by a flare is that it will set clothing on fire and, when the payload bounces off a person, set fire to anything flammable around them. For the storyline, I inferred the flare could penetrate the fuel line. That's not true.

I didn't transport Hwasong-16 missiles with liquid propellants because of the added weight, the corrosiveness of the fuels, and the temperatures at which the liquid hydrogen and oxidizer needed to be stored. Missiles are designed to burn either solid or liquid fuel. However, I couldn't find which the Hwasong-16 used because North Korea didn't publish technical data on this ICBM. Subsequently, I went with liquid fuel because it better suited my storyline. Had the missile used solid fuel, the manuscript would have changed slightly.

Paralytic shellfish poisoning (PSP) is as described. According to Australia's Department of Health and the Washington State Department of Health: *Bivalve molluscan shellfish such as clams, mussels, oysters, geoduck, and scallops can accumulate PSP. It's normal for biotoxin producing algae to be present in marine water. They are usually in low numbers that cause no problems. But when the algae "blooms," the amount of biotoxin-producing algae can increase. The increased algae become a greater food source for shellfish. The more algae the shellfish eat, the more biotoxin they accumulate. Biotoxins don't harm shellfish, so the level in their tissue will rise until the bloom subsides. When the number of toxin producing algal cells returns to normal low levels, the shellfish eventually flush the toxin from their bodies. It can be several days to several months or longer before they're safe to eat again.* Further information on PSP can be found at (https://www.doh.wa.gov/CommunityandEnvironment/

Shellfish/RecreationalShellfish/Illnesses/Biotoxins/ParalyticShellfishPoison) and (https://www1.health.gov.au/internet/main/publishing.nsf/Content/cda-cdi3701e.htm).

The description of the jungles in Sumbawa was embellished for the storyline's sake. In researching military jungle training exercises, I read an excellent depiction of "green hell" in an article by James Elphick. This was in the February 1, 2018 edition of *Military Life* and was the source of my embellishment as to what Tamala and Nabar encountered. The link to that article is (https://www.wearethemighty.com/military-life/why-jungle-warfare-school-was-called-a-green-hell). A good explanation of how the jungle interferes with current communications systems, and the new technology that's overcoming these limitations, can be found in an article by Thomas Withington in the March 24, 2020 edition of *Asian Military Review*. I used this to understand what communication issues Major Tamala would encounter. This article can be found at (https://asianmilitaryreview.com/2020/03/mumble-in-the-jungle/).

The multiple integrated laser engagement system, or MILES, used in the Sumbawa jungle training exercise functions as described. Laser transmitters are attached to each individual and accurately replicate the ranges and lethality of the weapons used. The system detects laser "bullet" hits and performs casualty assessments. Information on this system was taken from (https://fas.org/man/dod-101/sys/land/miles.htm) and (https://en.wikipedia.org/wiki/Multiple_integrated_laser_engagement_system).

To the best of my knowledge, North Korea doesn't have an island facility that manufactures weapons. They do send prohibited ballistic missile-related items on regularly scheduled Air Koryo and Iran Air flights to Iran in violation of UN sanctions. The origin of North Korea's missile program, and its exports to Iran, can be found in an undated 2021 article produced for the Nuclear Threat Initiative

(NTI) by the James Martin Center for Nonproliferation Studies at the Middlebury Institute of International Studies.

Iran possesses the largest and most diverse missile arsenal in the Middle East and can strike Israel and every middle eastern country. It's a significant hub for weapons proliferation—selling missiles to Hezbollah, Syria's al-Assad regime, Yemen's Houthi rebels, and anyone else willing to launch them at Israel or a country with differing geopolitical interests. In September 2019, Iran attacked Saudi Arabian oil facilities with cruise missiles, temporarily halting the production of seven percent of the world's oil. In January 2020, they launched twenty-two ballistic missiles at the Al-Asad Air Base west of Baghdad, inflicting Traumatic Brain Injury on more than one hundred United States military personnel. Further information can be found in an August 10, 2021 paper published by the Center for Strategic & International Studies for more information. This can be found at

(https://missilethreat.csis.org/country/iran/). A good primer on Iran's missile capabilities is in a March 2019 Brookings paper by Robert Einhorn and Vann H. Van Diepen, titled *Constraining Iran's Nuclear Missile Capabilities*. This can be found at (https://www.brookings.edu/research/constraining-irans-missile-capabilities/).

North Korea's sales of ballistic missiles to Iran have existed for some time. An excellent article that explains this can be found in *United Against Nuclear Iran*. I considered using more data from this article in my manuscript, but it slowed the pace of the novel. Here's the link:

(https://www.unitedagainstnucleariran.com/north-korea-iran#:~:text=North%20Korea%2C%20in%20tandem%20with%20China%2C%20sent%20a,frequent%20presence%20at%20North%20Korean%20ballistic%20missile%20test-launches).

Intelligence agencies generally agree that most of the missile technology obtained by Pyongyang came from Russian scientists who were employed at the Makeyev Rocket Design Bureau and, after the fall of the Soviet Union, found themselves unemployed.

Although North Korea offered them consulting jobs, the Russian government wouldn't allow them to leave the country. However, some found a way. According to a December 29, 2017 article by Tariq Tahir in *Mail Online*, a publication of *the Daily Mail* in Great Britain, they provided the technology that allowed North Korea to develop missiles capable of carrying nuclear warheads. For the sake of the storyline, China and Russia's contributions were abbreviated and simplified.

Israel does have a multi-layered missile defense system, which I summarized so as not to bog the reader down in minutia. More information on this can be found at (https://www.jewishvirtuallibrary. org/israel-missile-defense-systems#:~:text=Israel%2C%20in%20 collaboration%20with%20the%20United%20States%2C%20 has,warning%20system%20for%20incoming%20projectiles%20 in%20August%202017).

Very slender vessels, or VSV's, are frequently used by drug cartels. Having a speed of approximately twenty knots, they're difficult to detect because it's a semi-submersible that punches through the waves instead of riding on top of them. This gives it stability and speed even in heavy seas. For further information on VSVs, please visit (https://www.yahoo.com/news/colombian-drug-smugglers-built-stealthy-172409573.html).

Canggu is a friendly coastal village on the south coast of Bali, Indonesia. My apologies to the residents and local authorities for associating you with my fictional slimeball and his thugs. To the best of my knowledge, no smuggling or other illegal activities are centered there, nor are the police and residents on illicit payrolls. Instead, the village is a tranquil place popular with surfers for being one of Bali's few longboard-friendly surf spots. The description of Wirjawan's house was taken from a listing for a Canggu home. You can take a closer look at it by going to

(https://www.luxuryestate.com/p89216683-villa-for-sale-banjar).

Although Sapto Wirjawan is a fictional character, I mentioned he was involved in human trafficking because, just as in my novel

The Organization, I wanted to call attention to what continues to be a major problem in Indonesia. It's estimated that seventy to eighty thousand children are trafficked there per year, with an unknown number smuggled to Malaysia, Taiwan, and the Middle East. The most prevalent areas for these child abductions are in Bali and urban centers. Authorities need to get their act together because they only become involved when under pressure from the international community. Sadly, when this pressure subsides, so does their interest. More information on this subject can be found at

(https://borgenproject.org/child-sex-trafficking-in-indonesia/).

It's reported that North Korea has approximately one hundred twenty-three merchant ships operated by Ocean Marine Management Company (OMMC). Some of these ships are renamed from time to time to avoid international sanctions. Additionally, OMMC occasionally uses front companies in Hong Kong to act as surrogate owners of vessels to obfuscate North Korean involvement. These front companies include Trendy Sunshine Hong Kong Limited, SBC International, Advance Superstar (Hong Kong) Limited, and Shen Zhong International Shipping. The names of the vessels used in the novel are fictional.

The drone ViDAR system is as represented. Developed by Sentient Vision Systems in Melbourne, Australia, it provides optically autonomous real-time and wide-area search capabilities from unmanned aerial vehicles and manned aircraft. To the best of the author's knowledge, the MALE drone is not equipped with this system. I added this capability to give a plausible way to discover Wirjawan's VSV.

The information on SIGINT and reconnaissance satellites is accurate and taken from several media sources. These include an article by Eric Adams in the September 6, 2019 edition of *Popular Mechanics*, a January 19, 2019 article by William Harwood in *CBS News*, a September 30, 2020 article in *LiveScience* by Rafi Letzter, and a June 6, 2012 article by Craig Covault that appeared in *AmericaSpace*. Below are the links to those articles (https://www.popularmechanics.com/military/research/a28937898/kh-11-satellites/), (https://www.cbsnews.com/news/delta-4-rocket-boosts-classified-spy-satellite-to-space-vandenberg-air-force-base/), (https://www.livescience.com/secret-sattelite-details.html), and (https://www.americaspace.com/2012/06/06/top-secret-kh-11-spysat-design-revealed-by-nros-twin-telescope-gift-to-nasa/).

Manufactured by Lockheed, the last KH-11 spy satellite was launched on October 19, 2005, and soon after replaced by the KH-12. The KH stands for keyhole, referring to looking through the keyhole at someone. Most believe that this newer version allowed for "live" imagery viewing. These satellites are placed into orbit by a Delta IV heavy-lift rocket at the cost of approximately four hundred forty million dollars. More information on how US spy satellites have evolved can be found at (www.universe-galaxies-stars.com/KH-11.html).

The House of Leadership in central Tehran is the residence, bureaucratic office, and principal workplace of Iran's Supreme Leader. There is no indication that a meeting occurred there before the missile attack on the Ayn al-Asad airbase in western Iraq and another in Erbil. This was done to bring the NSA and its satellites into the storyline.

The ScanEagle drone operates above fifteen thousand feet and has a flight endurance of twenty hours. The Indonesian military uses it for maritime surveillance. To the best of my knowledge, it doesn't carry armament. Further information on this drone can be found in an article by Ronna Nirmala in the February 26, 2020 edition of *BenarNews*. The following is the link to that article (https://www.benarnews.org/english/news/indonesian/drone-deal-02262020162725.html).

Indonesia is one of only twenty-four countries with an embassy in Pyongyang, North Korea, and is said to have a cordial relationship with the hermit kingdom. The purported response of the military, the cabinet, and the president of Indonesia to North Korea's kidnapping of Wayan and Eka existed only in my mind and was done for the sake of the storyline.

The information on the NSA and Bluffdale, Utah, was taken from a fascinating article by James Bamford that appeared in *Wired* magazine. The link to that article is below. The Utah Data Center (UDC) is a heavily fortified complex in Bluffdale, which sits in a bowl-shaped valley with the Wasatch mountain range to the east and the Oquirrh Mountains to the west. The center is said to receive data from NRO satellites and cryptanalyzes or breaks unbelievably complex encryption systems employed by other governments and computers users who believe they've downloaded an off-the-shelf encryption program that not even the NSA can break. Wrong! Further information on this and the NSA can be found at

(https://www.wired.com/2012/03/ff-nsadatacenter/#:~:text=10%20 NSA%20headquarters%2C%20Fort%20Meade%2C%20 Maryland%20Analysts%20here,also%20building%20an%20 %24896%20million%20supercomputer%20center%20here).

Information on how the NSA uses its algorithms to prioritize data from its information sources and distributes it internally was invented for the storyline because the NSA doesn't divulge such information. Therefore, I made a guesstimate based on my research.

As described, Mossad is one of Israel's three major intelligence organizations and is responsible for intelligence collection, covert operations, and counter-terrorism. Its director answers only to the prime minister. Unlike other security agencies, its objectives, powers, and budget have not been defined by any law, thereby giving it a high degree of flexibility. It's estimated that seven thousand persons work within this highly compartmentalized organization.

The operating parameters of both the RQ-4 Global Hawk and MQ-9 Reaper are as written. As far back as 2006, DARPA had a sense-through-the-wall (STTW) system, which is believed to have been applied to military UAVs. Information on STTW was taken from a September 17, 2008 article by William Saletan in *Slate*.

This can be found at (https://slate.com/technology/2008/09/killer-drones-that-can-see-through-walls.html).

As represented, the Wide Global Satcom system (WGS) is a high-capacity United States Space Force satellite communications system. One WGS spacecraft has as much bandwidth as the entire Defense Satellite Communications System (DSCS). Further information on the WGS can be found at

(https://www.aerospace-technology.com/projects/wgs-satellite/) and

(https://www.intelligent-aerospace.com/military/article/16543766/global-hawk-reconnaissance-uav-to-receive-highspeed-satellite-communications-link).

The RQ-4 Global Hawk can remain airborne for approximately forty-two hours, although some sources will claim only thirty-two. The MQ-9 Reaper has an aloft time of fourteen hours. Additionally, the Global Hawk has a range of slightly more than fourteen thousand miles, while the Reaper is approximately one thousand one hundred fifty. The ceiling limitations are similar—the Reaper maxing out at fifty thousand feet while the Global Hawk is sixty thousand. Further information can be found at (https://www.af.mil/About-Us/Fact-Sheets/Display/Article/104516/rq-4-global-hawk/) and

(https://www.creech.af.mil/News/Article-Display/Article/697004/piecing-the-puzzle-together-rpas-provide-crucial-cap-capabilities-flying-the-mi/).

The drone base in Saudi Arabia exists. It was a secret until the *New York Times* published an article on its existence. However, it's unknown whether the Global Hawk flies from here. Further information on this base can be found at

(https://www.haaretz.com/.premium-u-s-drone-base-in-saudi-arabia-exposed-1.5229079).

The United States Air Force has five bases in Oman, which are located at al-Hasib, Siba, Markaz Tamarid, and Masir. It's unknown whether the MQ-9 Reaper is flown from them. I assumed United States drones were prevalent in a country just across the Gulf of

Oman from Iran. Since the Reaper costs "only" thirty-two million dollars and the Global Hawk around two hundred twenty million dollars, I believed Reapers would be far more prevalent in Oman.

Baledogle Airfield is a military airbase located in the district of Wanlaweyn in the Lower Shabelle region of Somalia. A former Soviet-built airport that serves as a base for the Somali Air Force, it's also used by the USAF to send drones against Al-Shabaab militants. Further information can be found in an October 4, 2018 article by Kyle Rempfer in *Air Force Times*. This can be found at (https://www.airforcetimes.com/news/your-air-force/2018/10/04/secret-us-base-in-somalia-is-getting-some-emergency-runway-repairs/).

The Global Hawk's processing, exploitation, and dissemination (PED) system is as described. It's unknown whether the sensors associated with this system can detect nuclear materials, but I believe that capability exists, and I included it in the storyline. Kris Osborne, the defense editor for the *National Interest*, authored an excellent article on the Global Hawk's surveillance abilities, which I incorporated into the story. This can be found at (https://nationalinterest.org/blog/buzz/how-us-air-force-global-hawks-will-serve-2040s-174942).

The Automatic Identification System, or AIS, is primarily used to allow ships to view maritime traffic in their area and be seen by that traffic. However, it's also used by fleet and ship owners to track the location of their vessels, by national authorities to monitor the fishing fleets of other nations, for search and rescue, and so forth. It's not uncommon for these devices to be switched off when convenient.

Israel is one of the world's largest exporters of UAVs, in terms of the numbers sold. The Eitan is manufactured by Israel Aerospace Industries (IAI). It costs thirty-five million dollars, and the operational parameters are as indicated in the storyline. Further information on this drone can be found at (https://en.wikipedia.org/wiki/IAI_Eitan).

An interesting segue is that, during my research, I discovered Abraham Karem is considered the founding father of UAV technology. An aeronautical engineer whose Assyrian Jewish family moved from Baghdad to Israel, he built his first drone during the Yom Kippur war. Later immigrating to the United States, he founded Leading Systems Inc. His company manufactured several drones, including the Amber, which evolved into the Predator. Although his company went bankrupt, it was purchased by General Atomics, who employed him to develop ultra-high endurance UAVs.

Israel has diplomatic relations with Ethiopia and provides them with military assistance. I had the Eitan drones refuel there because this aircraft doesn't have the range to fly from Israel, conduct a search for the platform in the Arabian Sea, and return—not even close. I needed to extend their range somehow. There's no indication that Israeli aircraft have used Ethiopia for military operations or had access to its airfields.

Tel Nof Air Base, also known as Air Force Base 8, is near Rehovat and is one of three principal airbases of the Israeli Air Force. According to a September 27, 2019 article by Arie Egozi in *Breaking* Defense, the mission of that base shifted in recent years from flying manned aircraft to drones. Eighty percent of all Israeli Air Force flight hours are by unmanned aircraft.

The Fordhow fuel enrichment plant was a former Islamic Revolutionary Guard Corp facility near the village of Fordhow—twenty miles from the city of Qom and deep within the mountain. It's believed the plant produces nuclear weapons and was constructed close to Qom because that city is considered so holy to Shia Muslims that attacking it might bring about a Shiite religious response.

A typical LNG tanker holds more than thirty-three million gallons of liquified natural gas, equating to twenty billion gallons of natural gas. For the sake of the storyline, I had the two F-35I aircraft survive the blast. However, an explosion of that magnitude would have a twenty-mile radius and destroy the aircraft.

The description of an electromagnetic pulse, or EMP, is accurate. Although it won't kill anyone, it will render useless any electronic circuit with which it makes contact. A good article on the effects of EMP was written by August Neverman in the March 30, 2019 issue of *Common Sense Home*. The description of the EPFCG, or explosively pumped flux compression generator, is accurate.

Although the submarine *Avenger* is fictional, the Israeli navy has six Dolphin-class submarines purchased from Germany and financed by them. They're armed with sixteen torpedoes and Popeye Turbo submarine-launched cruise missiles (SLCMs) that have a range of nine hundred thirty miles. Each missile can carry a two hundred kiloton nuclear warhead. You can look inside an Israeli Dolphin-Class submarine in the October 22, 2016 issue of *Submarine Matters*. It has excellent renderings of the sub's interior. The article can be found at

(http://gentleseas.blogspot.com/2016/10/israel-seeking-three-new-submarines.html).

The description of how a missile is launched from a submarine using a steam cannon is accurate and was taken from a February 13, 2007 article in *Popular Science* by David Hambling. You can find this article at

(https://www.popularmechanics.com/military/weapons/a25176/launching-missile-from-submarine/).

The receipt of the emergency action message, or EAM, by Manker and the use of the Sealed Authentication System, or SAS, was based on a modification of what the United States military used at one time to authorize a missile launch. An EAM directs forces to execute a specific action, with the SAS ensuring the message is authentic and unaltered. Further information can be found at (http://mt-milcom.blogspot.com/p/what-is-emergency-action-message-or-eam.html). The SAS is a three-by-five-inch plastic shell with a perforation down the center. It contains an opaque film with an alpha-numeric code imprinted on it. One "cracks" it in half to extract the opaque film to get at the code. More information can be found in a paper written by Jeffrey G. Lewis and Bruno Tertrais from the Middlebury Institute of International Studies at Monterrey. This can be found at (https://www.nonproliferation.org/wp-content/uploads/2019/02/Finger-on-the-Nuclear-Button.pdf).

The description of what occurs during a nuclear explosion was taken from an April 17, 2016 article by Ross Pomeroy in *RealClear Science*. The subjects of this article were Richard Feynman and Ralph Carlisle Smith. They witnessed the first detonation of a United States nuclear weapon without wearing dark protective glasses, although they saw the explosion from twenty miles away.

The description of ransomware is accurate. The explanation of this malware was taken from an article by Josh Fruhlinger appearing in the June 19, 2020 publication of *CSO*—which focuses on news, analysis, and research on security and risk management. It is part of ISG Communications. This article can be referenced by going to (https://www.csoonline.com/article/3236183/what-is-ransomware-how-it-works-and-how-to-remove-it.html).

The Quds are a part of the Iranian government that answers only to the ayatollah, meaning most in the government have no idea what they're doing. They're trained killers linked to planting roadside bombs in Iraq that have taken the lives of one hundred seventy US troops, the bombing of a Jewish community center in Buenos, the assassination of Iranian dissidents in Europe, and conducting other acts of terror around the globe. Additional information can be found in a February 14, 2007, ABC news article at

(https://abcnews.go.com/WNT/BrianRoss/story?id=2876019 &page=1).

As written, the Israeli government is actively trying to boost Arab tourism following the signing of the Abraham Accords with several Arab countries. The United Arab Emirates is one of the countries in which tourism is being promoted. For the storyline, I indicated that Qud assassins resided in neighboring Arab countries and lived there with a wife and children so that no one would suspect they were Iranian. With a forged birth certificate and other documents, they obtain another country's passport and conduct clandestine operations from there. However, there's no indication that the Qud does this, although they almost exclusively operate outside the country. Additional information on Arab tourism in

Israel can be found in a November 22, 2021 article by Ben Lynfield in FP at

(https://foreignpolicy.com/2021/11/22/israel-palestine-abraham-accords-arab-archaeology-national-park-propaganda/).

Santa Cruz, Bolivia, is the most dangerous city in that country. Pickpocketing and theft affect every part of the city of two and a half million people, with robberies at ATMs increasingly commonplace. The best hotels in that city are, as represented, the Mariott and the Radisson, which have an average rate of a little of one hundred USD per night. I took liberties in describing the airport ground transport facilities to get Ock into an SUV driven by Nabar. The airport is thirteen miles from the city, and deserted roads and jungle are not part of that urban landscape.

Active camouflage conceals an object from visual detection by rapidly adapting to its surroundings. There are several developing technologies the military hopes will accomplish this. One uses OLEDs, or organic light-emitting diodes, which projects images onto irregularly shaped surfaces, but currently works in only one direction at a time. This makes it critical to position the object to be camouflaged in the proper position relative to the observer. Another developing technology is phased-array optics, or PAO, which uses computational holography to produce a three-dimensional hologram of background scenery on the object to be concealed. The holographic image would appear to be the actual scenery behind the object independent of viewer distance or angle. However, all current active camouflage technologies are weakened by motion. Further information can be obtained at

(https://en.wikipedia.org/wiki/Active_camouflage).

ACKNOWLEDGMENTS

My sincere thanks to those mentioned below for their time and advice. Over the years, they've gotten to know the characters almost as well as me and provide insights and suggestions into their motivations, preferences, biases, and so forth. They're also not shy about giving me advice on how they believe the relationship between characters should proceed or who they'd like to kill off. For example, my mother-in-law, Shirley Goodburn, is so involved with the characters that she wants to see the manuscript as soon as I type the last period on the final page. Therefore, she gets it a few minutes before it's sent to my editor. In my defense, I would like to say that keeping your mother-in-law happy is a good thing.

Dr. Meir Daller, to whom this book is dedicated, has been a close friend and my physician for nearly two decades. He's humble, caring, and extraordinarily talented. If ever there was a modern-day Marcus Welby, for those who remember that television series, it would be him. I've incorporated his personality, mannerisms, and ability to communicate with others into several characters in my manuscripts. With great satisfaction, I'll leave who they are in the cloud. I would be remiss if I didn't mention that his wife, Dr. Rie Aihara, is an extraordinary medical talent who also projects humbleness, caring, and empathy towards others. Thank you both for what you do to make people's lives better.

To: Kerry Refkin, the glue for my novels—providing me with her invaluable editing, plot development skills, and cover selection.

To: The Group—Scott Cray, Dr. Charles and Aprille Pappas, Dr. John and Cindy Cancelliere, Shirley Goodburn, Carol Ogden Jones, Doug and Winnie Ballinger, Ed Houck, Cheryl Rinell, and Dr. Meir Daller for continuing to be my sounding boards. Thank you for your insights.

To: Zhang Jingjie for her expert research. There's no one better. Thank you, Maria.

ABOUT THE AUTHOR

Alan Refkin has written ten previous works of fiction and is the co-author of four business books on China, for which he received Editor's Choice Awards for *The Wild Wild East* and *Piercing the Great Wall of Corporate China*. In addition to the Gunter Wayan series, he's published the Matt Moretti-Han Li action-adventure thrillers and the Mauro Bruno detective series. He and his wife Kerry live in southwest Florida where he is working on his next Gunter Wayan novel, *The Defector*. More information on the author, including his blogs and the story settings for each novel, can be found at *alanrefkin.com*.